JAN PIEŃKOWSKI

The THOUSAND NIGHTS and One Night

Retold by *DAVID WALSER*

FOR
Staś and Naomi

Jan and David would like to thank
Sophie Bennett, Lois Bülow Osborne, Armin Müller,
Miriam Okarimia, Mateusz Stajewski, Andy Steward
and Jane Walmsley for their help

PUFFIN BOOKS
Published by the Penguin Group: London, New York, Australia,
Canada, India, Ireland, New Zealand and South Africa
Penguin Books Ltd, Registered Offices: 80 Strand, London WC2R 0RL, England

puffinbooks.com

First published 2007
This edition published 2011
001 – 10 9 8 7 6 5 4 3 2 1
Text copyright © David Walser, 2007
Illustrations copyright © Jan Pieńkowski, 2007
Made and printed in China
ISBN: 978–0–141–34070–8

CONTENTS

"Welcome" is a word the traveller hears constantly in Islamic countries – welcome to my shop, my restaurant, my home. *The Thousand Nights and One Night* provides the reader with a welcome too, this time to a more ancient Islamic world where magic is commonplace, animals talk and Genies rub shoulders with men. Here wicked sorcerers wreak havoc before getting their just desserts; treasure is lost and found, as is love. There are endless adventures to be had but also many lessons to be learned.

What is so unusual about *The Thousand Nights and One Night* is that it is a collection of stories within one story – that of the vengeful King Shahryar. Deceived by his first wife, he decides to take a new bride each evening and have her beheaded the following dawn. Enter Shahrazade, a clever, resourceful young woman, well-versed in the art of storytelling. She puts off her own death for a thousand and one nights by entrancing the King with gripping tales, stopping at a moment of suspense as dawn approaches. The King wants to hear more, so he stays her execution till the next day and the next . . . After three years of delay, he has fallen in love with her for her courage, wit and wisdom. He abandons his wicked resolve and all is well.

This clever use of a "framing" story enabled unconnected tales to be woven together over a period of some five hundred years. They were translated by an unknown Arab scholar and added to until they took their final form, probably in the 14th century. The earliest tales came from Persia and may date back to the 7th or 8th century. The later stories came from all over the Oriental world. In *Aladdin*, the Genie of the Lamp transports the Princess's palace from Cathay to Morocco – and back again. Sinbad the Sailor lived in Baghdad and set off on his voyages from Basra. *The Tale of the Fisherman and the Genie*, in which Muslims, Christians, Magi and Jews live in harmony, is thought to have come from Egypt. Happily for the Western world, the stories were collected and translated by a Frenchman, Antoine Galland, in 1704.

These retellings are from the translations of the Victorian explorer and linguist, Sir Richard Burton, some of whose own adventures rivalled those of Sinbad the Sailor for life-endangering perils and derring-do. They are, of course, for a modern audience, but they have lost nothing of their power to enchant.

It was our friend Sophie Bennett, herself a fluent Arabic speaker, who, on her rooftop terrace in Beirut, suggested that we should use the legendary translation by Sir Richard Burton for our retellings of these stories. On my return to London, in a dusty bookshop off the Charing Cross road, I found a Victorian edition in twelve volumes. It was exactly as Sophie had described: a learned, painstaking, literal translation from the Arabic, with wonderfully informative footnotes.

My own life has led me to many of the countries where the stories take place. Even before I was born, my parents met in what must have been part of King Shahryar's kingdom, for my father lost his fox terrier crossing the Khyber Pass on a hunting expedition. It was found days later by the next party to cross the pass, an English colonel and his wife who lived in Delhi. My father recovered his dog and married their niece. I was born in the Far East and the pain of parting from my adored Chinese amah, as we left Singapore just before it fell, is almost my earliest memory.

Travels have taken me through India, the Middle East and north Africa: I have watched the dawn rise across the jungle, seated on a howdah atop a swaying elephant in Bengal, and I have seen the sun plunging beneath the dunes near Ghadamis in the Libyan desert; I have sipped tea in the souks of Bukhara and Isfahan as carpet dealers rolled out their rugs and spun tales around the meaning of the designs; I have sketched the warriors on the friezes of Persepolis. In all these places I have tried to meet and talk to local people and to discover something of their lives – encounters that I hope have coloured my retellings of these tales.

That stories from so many lands can be combined into one narrative has long been a fascination, but it was brought home to me by an incident in the Libyan desert. A young man bade me welcome. When he told me he was Egyptian, I asked him why he welcomed me to a country that was foreign to both of us.

"We are all brothers," he replied.

David Walser

These stories were read to me as a small boy in Poland. In my childish mind, they became merged with stories of the Turks and the Tartars invading the country over the centuries and, if my features are anything to go by, leaving some of their genes in me. Ever since then I have wanted to know more about this mysterious eastern world – and it had to be at first hand.

Thanks to talking to people – be it my lifelong friend Dilip from Bombay; my Sikh computer merchant, Narindar, who has offered to teach me to tie a turban; my Chinese printer, Patrick, from Singapore; my Turkish tailor, Habibe, or Algerian barber, Hamid, from Hammersmith – more and more of the glittering pieces of the mosaic started to fall into place.

The tales seem to have pursued me down the years until I summoned up the courage to have a stab at doing them in pictures – at last an excuse for a grand tour of the fabled cities. They surpassed anything I'd imagined, as did the people. The Beiruti taxi driver who took us to Damascus turned out to have a wife to visit at each end of the rather long journey. Our Tartar guide got bitten by a dog in Samarkand and stoically concealed the wound until we arrived in Bukhara. Then there was the fleet of fearless smugglers in their tiny outboard-motored craft, setting off from Oman across the Persian Gulf with their cargoes of synthetic cloth and light bulbs, to return with boatloads of goats. In Luxor, Paul, our hotel porter, invited us to his domed dwelling for tea and sticky cakes, to the laughter of girls peeping out from behind the pillars. And in Marrakesh, Abdullah, the jovial maître d'hôtel, offered us lodgings in a grand house with a fountain in the courtyard where the staff left at night and locked us in.

This has been my dream job. As I travelled through these wonderful places I filled a score of sketchbooks with a thousand and one scribbles to jog my memory. As for the dappled, latticed light and shade, the brilliant splendour of the colours of the East, these are imprinted on my mind. I hope I have conveyed hints of them to you.

Jan Pieńkowski

The Teller of Tales
SHAHRAZADE
The First Night

There was once a powerful king in India who died and left two sons. Shahryar, the elder son, took over the Kingdom and sent Zaman, his younger brother, to be Shah of Samarkand. Both of them married and became model rulers, beloved of their peoples.

After twenty years had passed, King Shahryar longed to see his brother again, so he sent his Wazir, the chief minister, with precious gifts of horses bearing gem-encrusted saddles and white slave Mamelukes, to ask his brother if he would make the long and arduous journey to see him.

Shah Zaman was as delighted with the gifts as he was by the invitation and within three days he had set his Kingdom in order, preparing to make the journey. On the night before his departure, he said farewell to his wife and joined the expedition encamped just outside the city, ready to leave at dawn. Then, in the early hours, Shah Zaman remembered that he had left behind a most special gift he had set aside for his brother. He rose from his couch and went back to the palace. As he quietly entered his rooms, in order not to wake his beloved wife, he found her in the arms of a slave.

The Shah drew his scimitar and cut the two into four pieces with a single blow. Then he returned to his encampment and gave orders for an immediate departure.

Shah Zaman told no one of what had happened, but as he journeyed on, day by day, his health and spirits declined.

"How could my wife do this to me?" he kept repeating to himself.

By the time his brother came out to welcome him, he was a shadow of his former self. King Shahryar asked what ailed him but received no reply, so when they reached the palace, the King insisted on summoning the most skilful doctors to treat him.

A month later there was still no improvement in his brother's health. The King suggested a hunting trip, but Shah Zaman politely refused, so the King went without him. When the Shah was alone, he sat by the window of his room, which overlooked the King's private garden, brooding on how his wife had betrayed him.

Suddenly, he saw a gate in the wall of the garden begin to open. In stepped twenty slave girls with the Queen, his brother's wife and a model of loveliness. Shah Zaman drew back so as not to be seen as they passed under his lattice window on their way to a fountain that played into a great pool of water.

As they removed their veils, it was clear that ten of them were not slave girls at all, but male Mameluke slaves. Worse still, jumping down from a tree, a large slave walked boldly up to the Queen and embraced her. At sunset, the Mamelukes resumed their disguises and everyone left the garden.

Shah Zaman concluded that the betrayal his brother had just suffered was even worse than his own, for his brother was the King and the most important person in the land. Struck by this thought, Shah Zaman's melancholy began to lift.

The Shah drew his scimitar and cut the two into four pieces

The King returned ten days later. He was quick to notice the change in his brother, but despite his entreaties Shah Zaman would at first only agree to tell him the cause of his depression, and not the reason for his recovery. The King said to him, "Brother, you have to tell me how you got over such a calamity."

Reluctantly, Shah Zaman told him the whole story.

When the King heard how his own wife had betrayed him, he was so enraged that he had her put to death, together with all the slaves who had been with her in the garden. He swore that from that day on, he would take a new bride each night and have her put to death the following morning. In this way, he would never again risk being betrayed. Shah Zaman went back to his city with the same resolve.

And so from that day, as each night fell, the King's Wazir had to produce a beautiful maiden to spend the night with the King and in the morning have her put to death. This continued for the space of three years, until all the mothers who had not yet lost their daughters had taken them out of the city into hiding. Only the Wazir's own two daughters, Shahrazade and Dunyazade, were left. Imagine the Wazir's misery when Shahrazade said she would offer herself for the next night.

Shahrazade was a maiden of exceptional ability. She had read all the books she could lay hands on and was steeped in the legends of the past. She had studied the works of philosophers, scientists and poets. She was pleasant, wise and witty. She was also the apple of her father's eye, but she would not be changed in her decision.

In despair, her father said to her, "If you do not change your mind, I fear the same thing will happen to you that happened to the Ass."

"And what was that, Father?" asked Shahrazade.

And so her father told her the story.

The Tale of the Ox, the Ass and the Merchant

A merchant, rich in land and livestock, had been told by Allah how to understand the talk of animals, on condition that he did not share the secret with anyone else. Should he do so, he would die.

One day the Merchant was sitting near the stalls, playing with his children, when he heard the Ox complaining bitterly to the Ass.

"Look at you in that clean, sweet-smelling stall. I am woken when it is still night, yoked and taken to the fields, where I plough all day in the boiling sun. I come back to a filthy stable, sore and hungry. While you eat your fill of fresh hay, I survive on crushed straw."

"More fool you, you simpleton," replied the Ass. "When they bring you back to your filthy stall at the end of a gruelling day, you bellow and kick the stall and they take that to mean that you are contented. You should lie down and refuse to eat your poor meal. When they yoke you for the day's labour, you should refuse to move. After a couple of days, they will think you are ill and soon they will treat you a good deal better."

"You are my friend; I shall do as you say," replied the Ox.

So the next day, in spite of being beaten most thoroughly by the Ploughman, the Ox refused to pull the plough and lay down on the ground. When the Ploughman took him back to the stable, he refused his fodder. The Ploughman went to the Merchant to report that the Ox had fallen sick.

"Take that rascally Ass," said the Merchant, "yoke him to the plough and work him hard."

The Ass had never been worked so hard. By the time he got back to the stable in the evening, he no longer had the strength to hold up his head. The Ox, on the other hand, had enjoyed a peaceful day, lying in the stall, calling down blessings on the Ass. The Ox thanked the Ass warmly on his return.

"So, daughter," said the Wazir to Shahrazade, "be careful that you don't suffer like the Ass for lack of wits."

But to the Wazir's dismay, Shahrazade was not to be dissuaded.

The next day, the Wazir went sadly to the King to tell him of his daughter's decision. The King was much astonished for he honoured and respected his Wazir. He did not want to be the cause of Shahrazade's death, but he was not prepared to break his vow.

Now before Shahrazade went up to the King's bedchamber, she called her sister, Dunyazade, to her side. "Dunyazade," she said, "be ready. As the sun sets I shall call for you. When you come, beg me to tell you a new story to pass the sleepless hours before dawn. I will tell a tale that will one day be the saving of us and turn the King from his cruel ways."

And so it turned out.

When Shahrazade was received by the King she wept, and when the King asked her why she wept, she replied, "I should like to see my younger sister to take leave of her before the dawn."

The King agreed and when Dunyazade had come, she asked Shahrazade for a story, just as she had been instructed. The tale went on all night. As the cock crowed to announce the dawn, Shahrazade stopped her story. The King had listened enraptured and needed to know what happened next, so when the Wazir came in to take away his beloved daughter for execution, the King raised his hand to stop

him. "Wazir, I wish you to leave Shahrazade for another night. There is something I want to hear."

On the next night, Dunyazade came again to her sister's bedchamber and begged her to continue her story. With the King's permission, Shahrazade went on from where she had left off. But as the first cock crowed to herald the dawn, and the Wazir came woefully to take his daughter to her execution, once more she stopped her tale. As on the previous morning, the King raised his hand: "Wazir, I wish you to leave Shahrazade for another night. There is something I want to hear."

In this way, night followed night. As the shadows lengthened and darkness fell, Dunyazade came to her sister's side and asked her to continue her story. And so, for a thousand nights and one night, Shahrazade survived, and the tales of marvels that follow are just some of the stories she told.

The Tale of
ALI BABA
and the
FORTY THIEVES

There were once two brothers, Kasim and Ali Baba, who lived in a town in Persia. When their father died they shared what little had been left to them. Soon after, Kasim wedded the daughter of a rich merchant and lived a life of luxury. Ali Baba married the daughter of a poor man and lived from hand to mouth. By day, he would take his three asses to the woods near the town and gather dead branches to sell for firewood in the bazaar.

One day, Ali Baba had just finished loading up his beasts when he saw in the distance a dust cloud rising in the air. Soon he could make out a band of galloping horsemen and, fearing for his life, he drove the asses into the woods and climbed the highest tree he could find. Imagine his terror when the band of riders rode right up to the rocks below his hiding place! He watched them dismount and felt sure they were robbers who had come to hide the booty that he could see bursting out of their packsaddles.

Each rider tethered his sweating horse and unloaded his pack, while the Captain stood in front of the rock face and cried out, "Open sesame!" At this, a large rock swung back to reveal a cavern.

The Robbers entered and the rock closed behind them.

Ali Baba waited anxiously until the rock opened wide enough to let the Robbers out again. They all strapped their empty packsaddles on to their horses and set off at a gallop. Ali Baba climbed down and could not resist trying the magic words he had overheard.

"Open sesame!" he called, and back slid the rock to reveal a cavern filled with treasure. The moment he entered, the rock door clanged shut, but he was not alarmed for he was sure the same command would open it again. Glistening in the shafts of light that streamed in from holes in the cavern roof, he could see piles of jewels, as well as gold and silver coins, some in bags, some spilt out on the ground. As his eyes grew accustomed to the light, he saw fabulous brocades and embroideries, but he thought it wiser to take only gold coins, so he filled sacks with ashrafis and ducats.

"Open sesame!" he called and the rock face slid back. He loaded up his three asses, the rock closed and Ali Baba made his way home as quickly as he could.

At first his wife was sure he had robbed someone, so she was much relieved when he told her what had happened. She began to count the gold coins feverishly.

"Don't bother with that, Wife," he said, "just bury them where no one can find them." But she said she wouldn't sleep a wink if she didn't know how much gold was there, so she rushed over to her sister-in-law's house to borrow a pair of scales to weigh them.

Kasim's wife was curious to know why her sister-in-law should need the scales, so when she went to fetch them from the kitchen, she smeared sticky grease on both pans of the scales, hoping to find some telltale sign when her sister-in-law returned them. When she

Glistening in the shafts of light, he could see piles of jewels

did so later in the day, Kasim's wife found a small gold coin sticking to the shiny brass.

"Now you're a fine sort of husband," she complained to Kasim that evening. "You count your gold coins, but Ali Baba has so many, he has to weigh them!"

Kasim hardly slept the next night, so consumed was he with envy and greed. When morning came he lost no time in rushing round to his brother's house. Not wanting to have bad blood between himself and his brother, Ali Baba told Kasim the story of how he had come by the gold coins. And when Kasim said threateningly, "You had better tell me the whole truth, Brother, as well as the magic word," Ali Baba also told him the password.

Kasim wasted no time. The next morning, he hired ten asses and set off for the cavern. On the command of "Open sesame!" the rock face swung back, but then closed as he stepped inside. In the shafts of light streaming down from the cavern roof, he saw piles of jewels, heaps of gold and silver coins spilling out of bulging sacks, rich brocades and embroideries strewn all about. His eyes were swimming with wonder and excitement. Eager to load up his asses, he shouted out, "Open wheat!" but nothing stirred. He remembered that the password was some grain or other, so he cried out, "Open rye!", but again nothing stirred. "Oats, barley, corn," he tried everything he could think of, but still nothing stirred. All of a sudden, he heard the sound of horses' hooves and excited voices. The Robbers had returned. The rock clanged open, Kasim burst out of the entrance, trying to run past the Robbers, but he was cut down with one blow of a sword.

The Robbers were so alarmed that someone had discovered their treasure trove and knew the password to enter that they quartered Kasim's corpse and hung the four pieces just inside the entrance as a warning to anyone else who might enter.

When Kasim failed to return by nightfall, his wife went round to tell Ali Baba. She feared the worst and regretted bitterly that she had aroused her husband's jealousy of his brother. The sun rose and still Kasim had not returned. Ali Baba set out for the woods with his three asses and, when he reached the rocks, he saw traces of blood where the cave was hidden. Terrified by what he might find, he called out, "Open sesame!" The rock slid back, and there, either side of the entrance, hung his brother's body in four separate pieces. He took them down, wrapped them tenderly in sacking, ready to load on to one of his asses. It seemed a pity not to put his other two asses to good use, so he filled some more sacks with gold ashrafis and ducats, being careful not to be tempted by the rich brocades and embroideries. He called out, "Open sesame!" and the rock swung open again. Ali Baba loaded up the three asses with his brother's body and the bags of gold coins. He cunningly concealed everything under dead branches and set off for the town.

First he went to his own home where he left the two asses carrying the gold, instructing his wife to bury the coins with the others. He went on with the third ass to his brother's house and was met at the door by the slave girl, a sharp lass called Morgiana.

"Morgiana, a great tragedy has befallen my brother. He is dead, and you must prepare for the funeral rites while I go to break the news to my sister-in-law."

Ali Baba did his best to comfort his sister-in-law, though he had to tell her all that had happened. He said not to tell a soul outside their houses and that after the required period of mourning for her husband, he would take her as his second wife, look after her and make sure she was well cared for.

His brother's body hung in four separate pieces

Ali Baba left the grief-stricken widow in tears and went to find Morgiana. They made a plan together and, when Ali Baba returned to his own home, Morgiana set about putting the plan into action.

Morgiana called on the Apothecary and asked him for a medicine that might cure someone with a very serious illness.

"My master has eaten nothing for four days," she explained. "I fear he is near to death."

Next morning, she returned to the Apothecary and through her tears she said, "My master is no better. In fact, he is now so weak that he may not still be alive when I get back to the house."

The Apothecary gave Morgiana a more potent medicine, saying, "Calm yourself, girl. Go back quickly and give your master this potion with a little water. Come back to me if there is no improvement within the hour."

However, instead of going back to her master's house, Morgiana went off to find Baba Mustafa, an elderly tailor. After she had greeted him, she pressed a gold ducat into his hand and asked him to gather his needles and stout thread, and allow himself to be blindfolded; she would lead him to a place where there was an important job to be done. The old man hesitated, but when she pressed another coin into his hand, he agreed. Taking Baba Mustafa by the arm, Morgiana led him through the maze of streets until they reached her master's house. Only when they were inside a darkened room did she remove the blindfold. She told the tailor that her master had suffered a terrible accident and that his body was in four separate pieces which he, Baba Mustafa, would have to sew together in order to prepare it for the funeral.

As soon as he had finished, Morgiana said, "Now make a shroud to fit the dead man and you shall have more gold."

When all was done, Morgiana put the blindfold over the tailor's eyes and led him back to his shop. She rushed back home and, with Ali Baba's help, dressed the body in the shroud and placed it in a coffin. After the burial, Ali Baba remained in mourning for forty days before marrying his late brother's widow. Kasim's eldest son, a sensible young man, took over his father's shop.

Meanwhile, the Robbers were debating how anyone could have found out the secret password to their cave and stolen so much of their gold. To make matters worse, they saw that someone had now returned to recover the body of the man they had killed and quartered. One of the Robbers offered to go into the town to try to discover what man had recently died and been buried. He hoped this would lead him to the man who knew their secret.

Arriving early in the market square, in the disguise of a trader, the Robber found that all the shops were still shut except for one: at its door sat an old man stitching a shroud.

"I'm surprised you can see well enough to sew in this light, old fellow," he said to the tailor.

"I can see perfectly well, thank you," replied Baba Mustafa. "Why, only the other day I had to stitch up a man who had been cut into quarters, and that was in very poor light, I can tell you!"

"You're joking with me, of course," said the Robber, knowing he had found the very person to solve the mystery.

"Well, don't ask me any questions," answered the tailor. "I don't want to speak about it."

The tailor sewed together the four pieces of Kasim's body

The Robber placed a gold ashrafi in the tailor's hand and said soothingly, "Come, my good friend, there's another of these where this came from and all I should like to know is where you carried out this difficult task."

"That I cannot tell you; I was taken to the house blindfold and, when I had finished, I was led back here in the same manner."

"How strange!" said the Robber, quietly slipping the next ashrafi into the palm of the tailor's hand. "If I were to blindfold you, do you think you could remember how you went, and so find the place?"

Now when Baba Mustafa had been blindfolded and taken to Kasim's house, he had noted the number of steps he took, so he replied, "I think maybe I could."

Carefully counting his steps, Baba Mustafa led the Robber to the door of the house.

The Robber thanked the old man, took off his blindfold, marked the door with a piece of white chalk and went on his way.

Meanwhile, Morgiana came out of the door to go shopping and noticed the strange white chalk mark. She thought awhile and decided some enemy had made the mark, so she fetched a piece of white chalk and made the same mark on the doors of the neighbours' houses up and down the street.

When the Robber Captain heard that his man had found a clue to the mystery, he set off for the town. The Captain followed the Robber who had placed the mark on the door, but then they found the same mark on many doors and the Robber could no longer be sure which house was the correct one. The Captain was much displeased and, when they later returned to their forest den, the Robber was locked up as a punishment.

Another Robber volunteered to try his hand. He went to the bazaar, found Baba Mustafa, bribed him to lead the way to the house, made a mark – this time in

red chalk to make quite sure there could be no mistake – and went back to report to his captain.

When Morgiana stepped out of the house the next day, what did she see but a red chalk mark! She thought awhile and being of a suspicious nature, she made the same red chalk mark on all the neighbours' doors. The Captain returned and was again confused by so many similar marks. When he got back to the forest lair, he locked up the Robber who had made the red mark and decided that next time he would go himself. The Captain found Baba Mustafa, paid him handsomely, and was led to the house, but instead of making a mark, he looked up and down the street until he was sure he could remember exactly where the house stood. Then he went back to his forest lair to collect the other robbers.

With a new plan in mind, he sent one of his men to buy enough large mustard-oil pots to conceal the whole robber band, as well as one pot to be filled with mustard oil, and asses to carry them all.

When the man returned, the Robbers concealed themselves in the pots. They were told to climb out only when the Captain gave the command. Then the Captain smeared all the pots with mustard oil to make them look alike and loaded them in pairs on the asses. He disguised himself as a trader and drove the asses to the town, arriving just before nightfall in front of Kasim's house, where Ali Baba and his family now lived. Here he came across Ali Baba taking his customary evening stroll.

"Good sir," said the Robber Captain, greeting him, "I am from a nearby village and often come to sell my mustard oil in town, but this time I have left it too late and wonder if you would kindly let me stable my asses in your yard for the night and let me relieve them of their heavy loads."

The Robber Captain drove the asses to the town

Though Ali Baba had once seen the Robber Captain from the top of a tree, he did not recognize him because of his clever disguise, so he directed the man to a shed where he could stable his asses. Ali Baba called for Morgiana and told her to give the trader dinner and look after all his needs. He himself had planned to go to the Hammam baths in the morning, so he wanted her to make some broth for his return and tell Abdullah, the slave boy, to put out a suit of clean white clothes. Then he retired for the night.

After the Robber Captain had been given dinner by Morgiana, he went to the shed where his asses were stabled and whispered to his men that he would call at midnight to give them the command to break out of their pots. Until the midnight hour, the Captain stayed in his bedchamber and rested.

Meanwhile, Morgiana busied herself with her master's instructions: she started to prepare the broth, but no sooner had she lit the fire than the lamps ran out of oil and she could find no reserves so she called for Abdullah.

When Abdullah saw Morgiana fumbling about in the dark,

he said, "Why worry? The shed in the yard is stacked with oil jars. You could fill the lamps from one of them."

Morgiana thought this a good idea and went to the shed, but as she approached one of the pots she heard a voice from inside asking in a loud whisper: "Captain, is it time to come out?"

Morgiana started back in fright but, being a quick-witted girl, she realized what was behind this and, assuming the deepest voice she could muster, replied, "No, the time has not yet come."

She walked up to each pot in turn and when the Robber inside heard her coming and asked the same question, she gave the same reply. "Gracious me," she thought, "my master has let a band of robbers into his house!"

There was one pot from which no whisper came and Morgiana, seeing that this really was full of oil, filled her jug and returned to the kitchen. She replenished the lamps and lit them. Then she put a large cauldron on the fire and filled it with oil. When the cauldron was bubbling, she filled a bucket with boiling oil and, going back and forth to the shed, she poured enough into each pot to kill the Robber

inside instantly. When they were all dead, she went back to the kitchen, sat down by the fire and continued making the broth.

Just before the midnight hour, the Robber Captain rose from his bed and made the agreed signal from the window. No sound came from the shed. He called again. Still no sound. He called as loudly as he dared, but still no sound met his ears, so he crept past the kitchen into the yard and opened the shed door. Perhaps the men had gone to sleep, he mused. But when the smell of hot oil and burnt flesh assailed his nostrils, he put his hand on one of the pots: it was hot to the touch. He tried all the pots: they were all hot except for one. He realized what had happened. There was nothing left for him but to flee and, climbing over the wall, he went back to his forest lair.

Morgiana, who had heard the Robber Captain creep past the kitchen door, waited awhile to see if he returned and when he did not, she went to bed and slept soundly.

Ali Baba rose two hours before dawn and took himself off to the Hammam, knowing nothing of what had taken place in the night. He returned when the sun was well over the horizon and was surprised to see all the asses still in the shed. Why had the trader not gone to the market to sell his oil?

Morgiana led her master to the shed and asked him to peer into one of the pots. Ali Baba jumped back in horror when he saw a fully armed robber, but Morgiana explained that this man and all the others were dead. She took him to the kitchen to have the broth she had prepared and, while he drank it, she told him the story of what had passed in the night.

"And, Master, we must watch out for the Robber Captain. He may

Ali Baba jumped back in horror

still return. But for now, we must fetch Abdullah and bury all these bodies in the garden, so that no one sees them."

"You are a fine girl, Morgiana," said Ali Baba. "I am much pleased with you and I shall not fail to reward you."

Ali Baba and Abdullah dug a large hole in the garden under the tree, piled in the dead bodies and carefully levelled the ground. Over the course of the next few days, the asses were sold in small lots to different market traders, so as not to arouse suspicion.

The Robber Captain brooded in his forest den as to how he could be avenged. Once again, he had been outwitted, so he thought up a new scheme. He hired a shop in the bazaar, filled it with the finest materials from his treasure cavern and set up as a trader, calling himself Khwajah Hasan. By chance, his shop was opposite that of Ali Baba's nephew, which the young man had taken over after his father, Kasim's, death. It was not long before Khwajah Hasan got to know him, and he soon befriended him, showering the young man with attention and inviting him to meals.

Ali Baba's nephew felt he had to repay Khwajah Hasan's kindness to him, so rather than invite him to his own modest home, he asked his uncle if he would entertain the man at his house.

"Of course, Nephew," replied Ali Baba, "I should be delighted."

When the two of them arrived at Ali Baba's house the next evening, the master was outside, waiting to greet them.

"How kind of you," said Ali Baba, "to take such an interest in my nephew. Do please honour us by taking food at our table."

Khwajah Hasan insisted that he must leave, saying there was a special reason why he could not stay. When his host asked him what this could be, he said his doctor had told him he must eat no salt.

"That is no problem," said Ali Baba. "Morgiana has not yet started the meal and I shall tell her to use no salt in its preparation."

Without waiting for the man's reply, Ali Baba went to the kitchen to instruct Morgiana.

She was intrigued to know who this might be who wanted no salt, so when Abdullah went in to set the table and lay out all the food, she accompanied him as if to help. One look and she saw through the disguise: it was the Robber Captain. As he moved, she saw there was a dagger hidden in his robe. This then was the reason he wanted his food without salt: according to custom, a man may not kill someone whose salt he has just taken.

Morgiana went back to the kitchen to work out her plan. As soon as the party had finished eating, she and Abdullah brought in dried fruits and wine and then retired again. The moment for the Robber Captain to avenge himself on Ali Baba had almost arrived. Morgiana understood this and set her plan in motion.

She dressed in the clothes of a dancer, with a jewelled dagger at her waist, and told Abdullah to fetch the tambourine. Together they entered the room, asking if they could put on a little entertainment for the honoured guest. Ali Baba was surprised but pleased, especially when he saw how cleverly Morgiana danced. She took the dagger from her waist and wove patterns in the air. When the entertainment was over, Morgiana took the tambourine from Abdullah and, holding it in her left hand with the dagger still in her right, she went round the company for her reward.

Ali Baba threw in a gold coin, his nephew another. As Morgiana approached the Robber Captain, her dagger hidden beneath the tambourine, he fumbled for his purse. At that very instant, she struck, plunging the dagger into his belly. He fell down dead.

How cleverly Morgiana danced

"Oh, woe is me!" cried Ali Baba. "Why have you done such a dreadful thing, Morgiana? You will be the ruin of me!"

"No, Master," replied Morgiana. "This man was not a trader. He was not the oil merchant but the Robber Captain. He was about to kill you and that is why he would not eat your salt. Draw back his garment and you will see his dagger."

"Once again, Morgiana," said Ali Baba, "you have saved my life. This time, I give you your freedom and I shall wed you to my nephew." The young man was delighted, as was Morgiana.

Ali Baba, his nephew and Abdullah took the body of the Robber Captain to the garden and buried it with the rest of his band. Soon after, the young couple were married with great pomp and merriment. Their business flourished and when Ali Baba went to the treasure cave again there was no sign that anyone had been inside. The rest of the treasure was undisturbed and Ali Baba was confident that he was now the only person alive who knew the secret. He and his family lived in affluence from then on.

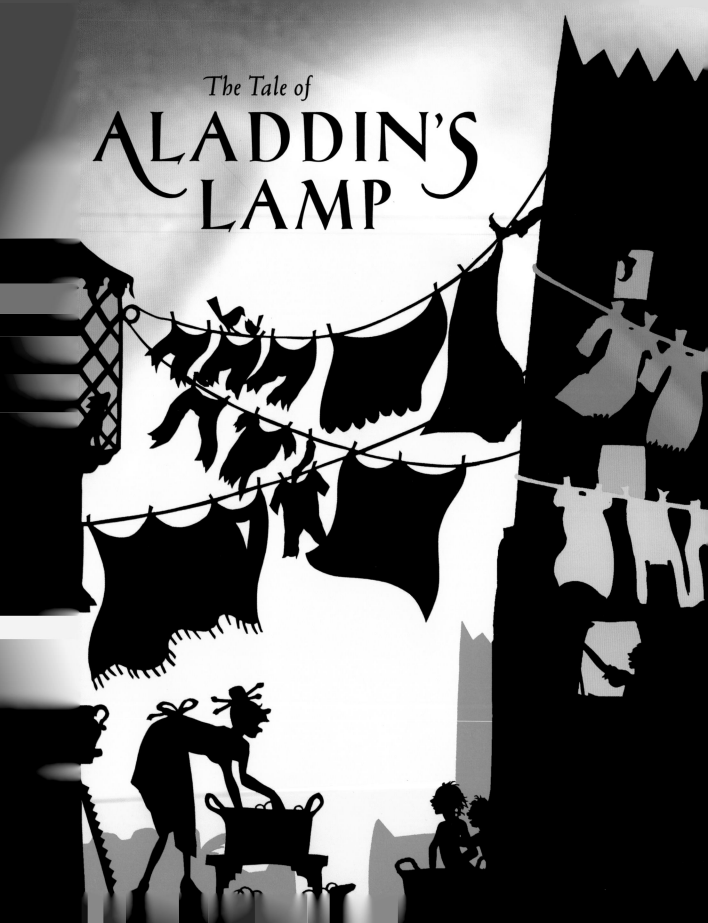

There was once, in a city of Cathay, a poor tailor called TuanKee, who had an only son, Aladdin by name. The boy was bright but wild and unruly. He would not obey his parents and only wanted to play with the street boys. When he reached the age of ten, the time had come for him to learn a trade; his father could not afford to apprentice him to anyone else so he took him into his own shop to learn the tailor's trade. But it was no good – the moment his father took his eyes off him, Aladdin was off to play with his friends. Punishment had no effect and the boy learnt nothing. Before long, his poor father fell ill with worry and died.

Aladdin's mother, the Widow TuanKee, had to sell the tailor's shop. She managed to make just enough money to feed herself and Aladdin by taking in washing. The boy was out all day, up to no good with his friends, and only came home for meals. They lived like this until Aladdin reached his fifteenth year.

Then one day a stranger came down the street where Aladdin was playing with his disreputable friends. He was a Dervish from a distant land, a monk who was also a magician. He had been travelling the world in search of Aladdin – the one person he needed to realize his devilish scheme. The moment he saw him, he knew this was the boy the stars had marked out.

The Magician drew one of Aladdin's friends aside and asked whose son he was. Then he hit on an idea. He rushed up to Aladdin, arms outstretched, saying, "Is it possible that you are the son of a tailor?"

Aladdin said he was, but that his father was long since dead, whereupon the magician began to sob noisily and threw his arms round the lad's neck.

"I have come all this way from my adopted land," he wailed, "to find my dear brother again and now you tell me he is dead. Although I left this city before he married, I saw his likeness in you immediately. You are my nephew and the consolation of my old age. Here, take these ten gold dinars and give them to your mother. Tell her that your Uncle Ebenezer longs to meet her and say I would like to dine with you both this evening. And, oh, by the way, just remind me again where you live . . ."

Aladdin kissed his new uncle's hand and rushed home to tell his mother, and to give her the gold coins. When she heard about Aladdin's strange encounter, she was amazed, for she had never heard her husband speak of having a brother, but she went off to buy the freshest vegetables and the most succulent meats the market had to offer. She borrowed some extra pots and pans from her neighbours and set about preparing a sumptuous meal.

When there was a knock at the door, they opened it to find the Magician accompanied by a slave bearing fruit and wine. Ebenezer greeted Aladdin and introduced himself to the Widow TuanKee.

There was a knock at the door

He began to question her about where his dear brother had sat and where he had done this and that. Soon he was wringing his hands, beating his breast, kissing the floor on which his brother had walked and prostrating himself in prayer until he fainted. Widow TuanKee was by now almost convinced that the man was indeed her dear husband's brother. She helped him gently to his feet, comforted him and seated him in the place of honour so that the feast could begin.

"Whoever leaves a son is not altogether dead," said Uncle Ebenezer and the good widow wept when she heard this. To distract her and to complete his deceit, he turned to Aladdin and asked him if he had mastered a trade.

Aladdin's mother answered for him, describing how he had wasted his years in idle play, how his father had died of grief and how the boy only came home to eat his meals, which she paid for by the sweat of her brow.

"How can this be, Nephew?" said Uncle Ebenezer, turning to the lad. "Why have you not learnt a trade to support your ageing mother? There are many other opportunities if your father's trade is not to your liking. I will buy you a merchant's shop, fill it with costly materials and set you up in business. You will become famous in the city."

Aladdin was delighted at this idea: he knew he would be able to dress in fine clothes and eat rich fare. The Magician could tell that the lad had swallowed the bait.

"But now, Nephew," he said, "you must prove yourself a man. Tomorrow, if Allah wills, I shall fetch you and we shall go to the bazaar to have a fine suit of clothes made for you. Then I shall find a shop to buy."

Widow TuanKee put aside her final doubts. How could he not be Aladdin's uncle if he was prepared to buy a shop for the boy and set

him up in
business? No stranger
would ever do such a thing.
She told Aladdin to obey his uncle
as if he were his father and to give up
his lazy good-for-nothing life and his
no-good friends. Then she got up, brought in the dishes and served
the homecoming banquet she had prepared. Uncle Ebenezer spoke
to Aladdin of business, man to man. When they had eaten and drunk
their fill, the Magician left.

At first light, he was rapping on the door again. "Come, Nephew.
We are off to the bazaar."

Uncle Ebenezer ordered splendid clothes for Aladdin and took
him to meet fellow merchants. He began to tell Aladdin about the art
of buying and selling. He even invited some of the merchants to a
meal, so that they could get to know his nephew.

Aladdin's uncle brought him home, tired but happy in his fine
clothes, with his new life opening up before him. Widow TuanKee
could hardly believe her eyes when she saw him smartly turned out
and already appearing more grown up.

"Tomorrow I shall collect you early to show you the sights of the
city," said Uncle Ebenezer.

Aladdin was so excited by what had happened to him in just one day that he hardly slept a wink. There was his uncle already rapping at the door to collect him and soon they were strolling through gardens, where crystal-clear streams meandered among trees and flowers. Aladdin laughed and joked with the Magician as though he had known him all his life.

When they reached the outskirts of the town, the landscape was becoming barren and uninviting. Aladdin wanted to turn back.

"What we have seen, my boy, is nothing compared to what I still have to show you," said the Magician. He entertained the young man with fantastic tales, a jumble of truth and lies, so that Aladdin forgot how tired he was.

"We have reached the place I spoke about," said the Magician when they came to a halt on a desolate hillside. "Have a rest and then fetch some sticks to build a fire. I shall show you wonders you have not even dreamt of."

When the fire had settled to a red glow, he took a pouch from under his cloak and sprinkled incense on it, muttering strange words in a low voice. There was a rumble of thunder and the ground heaved under their feet. Aladdin was so alarmed he tried to run away, but the Magician caught hold of him. He could not afford to lose him now so he struck the young man such a blow it almost knocked his teeth out. Aladdin wept with pain, but the Magician comforted him, saying he had not meant to hurt him, only to show Aladdin that he must now obey his uncle as if he were his father.

The Magician had arrived at his journey's end. When the ground erupted, it revealed a large stone with an iron ring in the middle.

"Under that stone," said the Magician, "is treasure enough to make both of us richer than any emperor or sultan in the whole world."

The Magician caught hold of him

Aladdin forgot his tears and tiredness and said he would obey his uncle, but he doubted he could lift the stone on his own.

"You must try," said the Magician. "Only if you raise the stone alone can we get at the treasure. Now, take hold of the ring and lift – but, while you do so, you must repeat your name and the name of your father and the name of your mother."

Aladdin did as he was told and the stone became as light as a feather in his hand. He laid it to one side to reveal a stairwell: twelve stone steps descended into pitch-darkness.

"Now, Nephew," said the Magician, "listen to me carefully. Here are my instructions – follow them to the letter. At the foot of these twelve steps you will find four rooms. In each room there are four urns of gold and silver, but you must not touch them or even brush against them. If you so much as stop, you will be turned to stone. In the fourth room there is a door. Speak your name, your father's name and your mother's name, and the door will open into a garden filled with fruit trees. At the far end, you will find a spacious alcove with a ladder leaning against the wall. The ladder has thirty rungs; when you have got to the top, unhook the oil lamp you will see hanging from the vault, put out the flame, pour away the oil and then bring the lamp to me. On your way back you can pick anything you like from the trees, but do not let go of the lamp."

Then the Magician put a seal ring on Aladdin's finger and said, "This ring will protect you from fear or harm, as long as you follow my instructions to the letter."

Aladdin went down the twelve stone steps, through the four rooms, past the urns, which he was careful not to touch, into the garden, past the fruit trees without stopping until he reached the ladder and unhooked the lamp. He put out the flame, poured the oil away, carefully placed the lamp in a pocket and started back.

The garden was a dazzling sight and the fruit trees were festooned with glittering stones. He recalled his uncle saying that he could now take what he wanted, so he filled his pockets with all the jewels he could reach. He did not realize what they were, but thought they might be fun to have. He even filled the pocket that held the lamp. He was so weighed down that when he reached the steps, he found he could hardly climb them.

Ebenezer was at the top, peering down, and when Aladdin saw him he said, "Please help me, Uncle, I'm too weary to climb all these stairs." But the Magician refused to help.

"Nephew, you must do it alone. If I so much as help you up one step, we shall lose everything. But I tell you what: just pass me the lamp and that will make it easier for you."

Aladdin knew that the lamp was buried under a pile of those nice bright trinkets he had picked off the trees. If he tried to pull the lamp out, he might lose some of them, so he said, "No, Uncle, I'll manage by myself if I have to."

"Just hand me the lamp anyway, Nephew. It will be so much easier for you," and the Magician eagerly reached out his hand.

"No, no, Uncle, I'm nearly there. I'll give it to you when I get to the top." He took another step upwards.

When the wicked Magician saw that he was not going to get his hands on the lamp before Aladdin had reached the entrance, he flew into a rage. He threw the rest of the incense on the fire and summoned the thunder. The heavy stone rumbled back into place, sealing the entrance, and the earth closed above it.

In one moment of unbridled anger, the wicked sorcerer had lost the treasure he had come so far and worked so hard to get. "At least," he thought, "Aladdin will starve to death and not benefit from the treasure." Then he set off back to his own country.

Too late, the truth dawned on Aladdin: his uncle was not his uncle, but a wicked sorcerer who had only wanted to get his hands on the lamp. He was overcome with terror and misery. Hours and, for all he knew, days passed. At first he wept. Then he prayed. Then he promised never to do anything wrong again and to work hard to support his mother by honest toil if only Allah would let him out of this dark cave. Once, when he was weeping, he began to wring his hands and by chance he rubbed the ring that the evil sorcerer had given to him earlier.

In a flash, the Genie of the Ring appeared. "Salaam! I am your slave. Your will is my command."

Aladdin trembled all over – the Genie was a terrifying sight. But he recalled what the Magician had told him about the power of

"Salaam! I am your slave."

the ring, so he took courage and said, "Genie of the Ring, deliver me from this place and put me on the earth again."

Hardly were the words out of his mouth when he found himself sitting outside in the sun, on the sweet-smelling grass. He had been in the darkness for so long that at first he could not bear to open his eyes. Little by little he opened his eyelids and he looked down again on the distant city. He made his way home to his mother, who was by now half crazed with worry. Her son had been gone three days and three nights.

When she saw Aladdin coming through the door, she burst into tears, flung her arms round his neck and thanked Allah for his safe return. After resting awhile, he had something to eat and drink and then he told her what had happened to him.

"All the wicked sorcerer wanted was an old lamp. If I had given it to him, he would surely have killed me. As it was, he left me to die of starvation in an underground cave. The lamp is at the bottom of this pocket," he added, tapping his side. "And I've got all these pretty trinkets for you, which I picked off the fruit trees."

Aladdin emptied his pockets and the gems filled two bags. Neither Aladdin nor his mother had any idea of their worth. As for the lamp, she placed it on a shelf. By now, the boy's eyes were closing with fatigue, so she put him to bed.

When he woke up, he was hungry, but there was no food in the house and his mother had no money, so Aladdin said to her, "Hand me that lamp, Mother; I'll go to the brass market and sell it."

His mother took down the lamp from the shelf but thought it would fetch a better price if she gave it a good polish. She had hardly given it the first rub when a gigantic green genie appeared. It seemed to fill the room.

"I am the Genie of the Lamp. What is your wish? While that lamp is in your hands, there is nothing I cannot do for you."

Poor Widow TuanKee swooned on the spot, but Aladdin, who had already been saved by the Genie of the Ring, jumped up from his bed and picked up the lamp.

"Genie of the Lamp, we have no money to buy food and we are hungry. Bring us something tasty to eat."

The Genie was gone, but reappeared in the twinkling of an eye bearing a tray laden with twelve shining dishes heaped with spicy meat and mouth-watering delicacies. The Genie set the food down in front of Aladdin and vanished.

Aladdin sprinkled his mother's face with rose water and placed perfumes under her nose until she came to.

"Get up, Mother. Look! Here is food and drink, which Allah has provided for us."

The good widow saw the burnished tray and all the rich fare that seemed more suited to a king's table, and was speechless. Only after they had eaten their fill did he tell his mother how she had fainted when the Genie of the Lamp appeared and how the Genie had granted his wish.

Widow TuanKee was all for throwing the lamp away, and the ring as well, saying they would only bring trouble upon their house, but Aladdin reminded her they had saved his life and brought them food when he and his mother were penniless and hungry.

"No, Mother, I shall never take off the ring. However, to please you, I shall hide the lamp so that you can't see it, only we must never tell anyone about it."

For two days, they lived on the food the Genie had brought them. When there was not a morsel left, Aladdin went to the market with one of the brightly shining platters, hoping to sell it. He did not know that it was solid silver so he asked a shopkeeper what he would pay for it. The shopkeeper saw that the dish was of the finest quality silver and, wanting to discover if the young man knew this, he asked cannily, "And what do you want for it, my son?"

"You know what it is worth," Aladdin answered.

The trader was not sure what to make of this clever reply, so he pulled out a gold dinar, which Aladdin accepted. Then the trader realized the lad had not known the true value of the dish and regretted he had not offered much less.

In order to turn the gold coin into coppers Aladdin went to the baker. He bought a loaf of bread and gave the change to his mother when he got home. She bought everything else they needed at the market. But soon the food ran out again, so Aladdin took another shiny dish to the shopkeeper. Week by week, Aladdin brought him one of the dishes, until all twelve were gone, and the tray as well.

One day there was no money left. There was nothing for it but to ask his mother to leave the room, take the lamp from its hiding place and summon the Genie.

"What can I do for you, Master?"

"Genie," said Aladdin, "can you bring us another tray of tasty food for we are half starved again?"

"To hear is to obey," said the Genie and vanished, instantly reappearing with a silver tray stacked with enticing dishes and jars of wine. Delicious smells of spiced meat and saffron rice filled every corner of the room.

Aladdin called his mother. "Look at this, Mother. You asked me to get rid of the lamp and now see what it has done for us."

They thanked Allah and ate their fill. There was enough left over for the next day, and when that was gone Aladdin tucked one of the shiny dishes into his clothes and went off to sell it.

It happened that his way took him past the door of an old silversmith, who was an honest man. He had seen Aladdin selling objects to the unscrupulous tradesman and was sure the lad was not getting a fair price, so he held up his hand and stopped him.

"Just a moment, young man. I have often seen you taking something for sale to that shop across the road. I fear the owner may be cheating you. If you are on the way to him again, why don't you show me what you have for sale? When I tell you how much it is worth, you can decide whether you will sell it to him or to me."

Aladdin agreed and handed over the dish. The silversmith saw that it was of the finest silver.

"Young man, is this dish similar to the ones you have sold before?"

"Yes," said Aladdin.

"What did that man give you for them?"

"One gold dinar for each."

"Young man, you have been cheated. I have weighed the dish and I would give you seventy gold dinars for each one."

From that day on, Aladdin and his mother were comfortably off but did not alter the way they lived too much. Aladdin was now growing up and no longer enjoyed the company of his ne'er-do-well friends. He liked to go to the markets and speak with the traders, learning about the value of the things that people bought and sold. Soon, he even began to do some trading himself and so he learned the worth of silver and gold objects as well as gems and precious stones. He became more knowledgeable by the day and it was not long

before he realized that the glittering ornaments he had picked off the trees in the underground cave were not worthless pretty baubles, but jewels and gems that would be the envy of kings.

One day, as Aladdin was setting out for the bazaar, he heard the town crier calling on all the citizens to close their shops and stay at home because the daughter of the Sultan, Princess Badr al-Badur, was coming to the Hammam baths to bathe. If anyone disobeyed this command, they would be put to death.

Aladdin had heard that the Sultan's daughter was like a perfect pearl and as radiant as the sun, so he was determined to get a glimpse of her if he could. He went straight to the Hammam and concealed himself in a doorway across from the entrance.

It was not long before the Princess and her court arrived and, as she entered the Hammam, she raised her veil. For a fleeting moment, Aladdin saw her face and the vision took his breath away. The young woman was more beautiful than any pearl and the sun was no match for her radiance.

As all the other women Aladdin had seen before kept their faces veiled, he thought that all women looked like his mother. Now that he had seen the Princess, he could think of nothing else and he made up his mind to marry her.

When Aladdin's mother heard of his ambition, she was sure he had taken leave of his senses.

"How can you possibly think that a poor tailor's son could win the hand of the Sultan's daughter? The Sultan would not accept a proposal from a prince if he were any less noble than his own family. How would you even make your proposal known to her?"

"Mother, you are the person who loves me more than anyone else,

so you will make my petition. If you do not agree to do so, I shall go mad. Only you can help me."

"Son, son, you are dearer to me than my right hand and I will do anything I can to help you and indeed to find you a bride, but let me look for someone among our equals. Even then her people will ask me if you have land or a business, and how shall I reply? If I can't answer poor people like ourselves, how can I answer the Sultan of Cathay, who has no equal in the land? They might even kill me or lock me away, thinking I was a mad woman."

Aladdin saw the wisdom of his mother's words, but also remembered that he had a present of amazing value. He told his mother that he had discovered the real worth of the glass ornaments he had picked from the trees in the cave, and that no king had jewels as valuable. When Aladdin had filled a bowl and arranged the gems to look their best, his mother was half blinded by the dazzling light. She knew that he spoke the truth, so she tried other arguments.

"If they wanted to honour me for this gift and I say I want my son to marry the Princess Badr al-Badur, won't they ask what estates you have and what is your income?"

"Mother, when they see the value of these stones, they will not bother you with trivial questions. We will face the problems as they come. Remember, the lamp will teach me what to do."

Early in the morning, his mother took courage and set off for the palace, the bowl covered with a clean kerchief and hidden under her robe. She arrived in such good time that she found a place for herself at the front of the audience chamber, which soon filled up with lords, chieftains, high officials, emirs and notables. The Sultan entered, took his place on the throne and bade them sit down to await their turn. The petitioners went up to him in the order of their station so, although the Widow TuanKee had been the first to arrive, at the end of the day she had still not been called.

She went home and told Aladdin what had happened. But her determination grew and every day she made her way to the palace; she arrived early and stood in the front row. One day on his way out, the Sultan asked the Grand Wazir what that old lady wanted.

"And I wonder what it is she is carrying under that kerchief," he added. "Bring her to me now."

Aladdin's mother was taken before the Sultan. She prostrated herself before him, kissing the ground. When the Sultan asked how he could help her, she had the courage to ask him to give his word that he would not punish her for what she was about to say. He agreed, promising in the name of Allah, and ordered everyone to withdraw except for the Grand Wazir.

The Widow TuanKee then told the story of how her son had hidden by the entrance to the Hammam, how he had seen the Princess Badr al-Badur without her veil and fallen hopelessly in love with her.

"Aladdin is my only son, great Prince, and he says he will kill himself unless he can win her hand in marriage. He would not rest until I had petitioned you."

The Sultan looked at the old lady kindly and laughed out loud. "And what might you be bringing me in that bowl?"

The Widow TuanKee held the bowl out and removed the kerchief. The shafts of light leapt from the gems and flashed about the audience chamber. At the sight, the Sultan and the Grand Wazir were at first speechless.

When the Sultan had recovered his wits, he said, "Not in all my days have I seen anything like this. I have nothing in my treasury that could match what I see here." He turned to the Grand Wazir, who agreed with him.

"The man who sends me such a gift deserves my daughter's hand."

The Wazir heard these words and was much displeased, for the Sultan had an understanding with him to let his daughter marry the Wazir's son. "Great Sultan, why not ask her to bring you forty golden platters heaped with jewels, each carried by a damsel attended by a eunuch slave?"

"An excellent idea," said the Sultan and, turning to the old lady, he made his new demands.

The Widow TuanKee went slowly back to her home, but when she told Aladdin what the Sultan had asked for, Aladdin smiled.

"I had expected him to ask for much more. Go out and buy some dinner for us, Mother, and I'll think of what to do."

Aladdin went to his room, took down the lamp and rubbed it. The Genie whirled up in front of him.

"What do you want of me, Master? Your will is my command."

Aladdin gave the Genie his instructions.

Imagine the widow's surprise when she returned to find her house bursting with girls so beautiful they would have broken the will of an anchorite, as well as their attendants and all the golden platters piled up with rubies, emeralds and diamonds.

The people of the town watched in awe as the procession, headed by Aladdin's mother, wound its way through the streets to the palace.

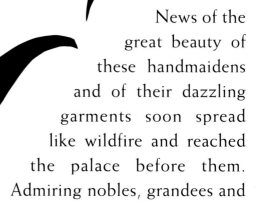

News of the great beauty of these handmaidens and of their dazzling garments soon spread like wildfire and reached the palace before them. Admiring nobles, grandees and

officials
were waiting
to receive them
and to admit them
to the Sultan's presence.

The gems near blinded the Sultan and his attendants with their sparkle, but it was the beauty of the maidens that most disturbed him. For some moments, he was struck dumb.

The Widow TuanKee stepped forward, greeted the Sultan and presented the gift from her son, assuring him that the Princess, his daughter, was worth many times what she brought, but that she hoped the Sultan would now allow Aladdin to wed his daughter.

The Grand Wazir was fuming and suggested further delays to the marriage, but this time the Sultan would have none of it. He was especially glad to see that his daughter, who had been so gloomy, was smiling with joy at the sight of all this magnificent treasure.

Then there were all these lovely damsels. He also saw that his Wazir's face was etched with envy.

The Sultan bade the Widow TuanKee return to her home and fetch Aladdin. He was eager to meet his future son-in-law and he was happy for the marriage ceremonies to start that very evening. The good widow ran back so fast that when she found Aladdin she could not utter a word, but he could see that all had turned out as he had hoped and he gave thanks to Allah. He kissed his mother's hand and also thanked her when she had given him a full account. Then he went to his room to summon the Genie. He asked to be taken to the most luxurious Hammam that had ever existed and there to be dressed in the finest robes.

"To hear is to obey, my lord," and Aladdin found himself whisked away to a Hammam whose walls were made of alabaster and cornelian, where he was bathed and dressed in robes that would have pleased a king. He then returned to his home.

"Do you require anything else?" asked the Genie of the Lamp.

Indeed Aladdin did. He must have an escort to the palace of forty-eight Mameluke slaves to attend him, mounted on fine horses – twenty-four to ride in front of him and twenty-four behind. Each was to carry a purse of a thousand gold dinars, which they were to distribute to the townspeople. His mother was to be finely dressed and attended by a dozen pretty maidens fit for a queen. He himself was to be mounted on a matchless Arab stallion.

In the twinkling of an eye, the procession was waiting in front of their house and soon set off through the town. The townsfolk knew that Aladdin was the son of a humble tailor, but they were proud of the handsome figure he cut and they liked his generosity, for the Mamelukes distributed the gold dinars as they went along.

Aladdin was mounted on a matchless Arab stallion

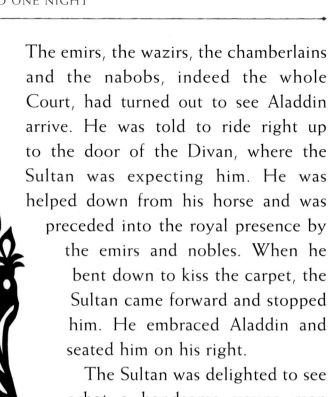

The emirs, the wazirs, the chamberlains and the nabobs, indeed the whole Court, had turned out to see Aladdin arrive. He was told to ride right up to the door of the Divan, where the Sultan was expecting him. He was helped down from his horse and was preceded into the royal presence by the emirs and nobles. When he bent down to kiss the carpet, the Sultan came forward and stopped him. He embraced Aladdin and seated him on his right.

The Sultan was delighted to see what a handsome young man he had chosen for his daughter and he listened with delight to Aladdin's most respectful and eloquent thanks. As their talk progressed the Sultan liked Aladdin better by the minute and it was not long before he ordered the marriage contract to be drawn up. The Sultan would have liked Aladdin to move to the palace that night, but Aladdin had other plans in mind.

He asked the Sultan for a piece of land in the palace grounds to build a pavilion worthy of his bride. "Yes, certainly," said the Sultan and pointed to a site opposite his palace.

Aladdin wanted to complete the new pavilion before his first night with his bride but said there would be no delay. The Sultan agreed and the marriage bonds were sealed.

Aladdin summoned the Genie: "Genie, I have a most important wish, that you build me a pavilion facing the Sultan's palace in the shortest possible time. It must be a true marvel, worthy of my wife, the Princess Badr al-Badur, and fitted with everything we need."

"Your wish is my command, my master," said the Genie.

The next morning, before the sun had kissed the rooftops, the Genie went to Aladdin and told him the pavilion was finished. "If you would like to inspect it, get up now and I shall take you."

It was a gracious pavilion, made entirely of jasper, alabaster, Sumaki marble and delicate mosaic work. Aladdin was shown the fine fittings and furniture: rugs from Cathay and Arabia; a dinner service of Ming porcelain; utensils of gold and silver. The stable was stocked with Arab horses in fine fettle, with pearl-studded saddles. Eunuchs and handmaidens, whose beauty would have seduced a saint, were ready to wait on him.

The most striking feature of the pavilion was an airy belvedere, a tower that rose above the level of the rooftop. It had twenty-four windows, each encrusted with emeralds, rubies and other gems. Aladdin was highly pleased, but turning to the Genie of the Lamp he said, "There is still one thing left to do. I want a carpet of the finest wools to stretch from the Sultan's palace to this pavilion, so that the Princess Badr al-Badur will not have to dirty her slippers."

"To hear is to obey." And it was done.

The turrets of the Sultan's palace were already warmed with the morning sun when the Sultan rose from his bed, yawned, stretched his arms and walked to the window. He threw open the shutters and could not believe what he saw. He rubbed his eyes, opened them even wider, but it was still there: an elegant pavilion, catching the rays of the rising sun. Slowly it dawned on him that this was the pavilion that Aladdin had promised.

When the Grand Wazir came to the royal bedchamber, the Sultan called him to the window.

"There you are, just look at that dazzling sight," he said. "Now do you see what a good match we have made for my daughter?"

But the Grand Wazir was filled with envy and malice. He replied, "No one could have built such a palace in one night unless by magic," and he considered how he might be avenged.

When, shortly afterwards, Aladdin arrived at the Sultan's palace, the Sultan kissed him on both cheeks and sat him down on his right, still holding his hand, while they chatted until the noonday meal. This was the formal start of the marriage ceremony.

The nabobs of districts and the governors of provinces had come from afar to witness the wedding and join in the celebrations. Everyone gazed in wonder at the beauty of Aladdin's pavilion.

When the sun had lost its strength, the Sultan rode down to the Maydan plain with his army officers, emirs and wazirs to show off their horsemanship. Aladdin followed on his Arab stallion and he outshone the best riders. The Princess watched from a balcony and fell madly in love with him.

The Sultan was not to be outdone and ordered a magnificent procession to escort his daughter to the pavilion. Aladdin's mother was next to the Princess Badr al-Badur as they walked along the

beautiful carpet that joined the palace to the pavilion and she guided her to the Princess's own apartment. Only then did the Princess lift her veil, and the Widow TuanKee understood why her son had been so smitten. The girl was indeed beautiful beyond belief and more radiant than the sun.

Meanwhile, in a far country, the wicked Magician Ebenezer daily boiled with rage that he had not got hold of the lamp after going to so much trouble and travelling to such a distant land. It was some consolation that Aladdin had died a miserable death, or so he thought, until one day he decided to check by casting his magic sticks. Oh, horror! Aladdin was not in the cavern. He quickly cast the sticks again to see the whereabouts of the lamp, and the lamp was not in the cavern either.

It took him only a short time to discover that Aladdin had in fact escaped with the lamp, that he had become immensely wealthy and married the Sultan's daughter. Ebenezer could not sleep a wink, he was so seething with fury and jealousy. He decided he had to set out yet again to try to recover the lamp.

After a long and arduous journey, the Magician once more entered the gate of Aladdin's city. As he wandered the streets, people seemed to talk of little else but the magnificence of the pavilion that Aladdin had built, how handsome the young man was and of all his many excellent qualities.

When Ebenezer saw the pavilion, he knew it was the work of the magic lamp and he schemed how to get hold of it and wreak his revenge. He found a coppersmith and ordered a large quantity of new lamps, as many as he could carry. When he had collected them, he set off around the streets of the city, crying aloud, "New lamps for old. New lamps for old." The people thought he was a madman and

soon there was a jeering, taunting crowd of children following him.

It so happened that the Princess Badr al-Badur, who was sitting in a niche at the front of the pavilion, heard the cry, so she asked her slave girl, Zuleika, to find out what it was about. She came back to tell the Princess there was a man offering new lamps for old, followed by a crowd of teasing children. The Princess laughed at such a strange tale. Zuleika had noticed Aladdin's old lamp and she told the Princess, who thought that here at last was a way in which she could show her gratitude to Aladdin for all he had given her.

"Zuleika, fetch the lamp," she commanded and, when she was given it, she sent Zuleika to exchange it for a shiny new one, thinking the dealer must have lost his wits.

The moment the wicked Ebenezer clapped eyes on the old lamp, he handed over a new one and dropped the rest for people to help themselves. This was the lamp he had sought for so long. He walked quickly away until he found a deserted spot. There he rubbed the lamp and the Genie appeared in front of him.

"What is your wish, Master? Ask what you want of me."

"Genie, I want you to transport me and Aladdin's pavilion, and all who are in it, to my homeland in Morocco."

"To hear is to obey." And it was done.

The following morning, as soon as the sun had risen, the Sultan got out of bed, stretched his limbs and walked to the window. He threw open the shutters to look across at his beloved daughter's pavilion, only to see a flat, empty plain, just as it used to be. And where was his beloved daughter? Frantically, he summoned the Grand Wazir.

"Now, Master, you understand why I told you that the pavilion could only have been built by black magic," said the Wazir.

He handed over a new lamp

The Sultan was too cross and distressed to listen and asked for Aladdin. Aladdin had gone hunting, so the Sultan issued orders for him to be brought back in chains. The Aghas and the senior army officers set off immediately and, when they at last found Aladdin, they explained to him their sad duty.

Aladdin asked them if they knew the reason for this sudden turn of events but they had no inkling, so he said, "Well, you must do as you are commanded."

So he was shackled and brought back to the Sultan. Aladdin was very popular among the townsfolk and when they saw him being led in shackles through the streets, they fetched their weapons, poured out of their houses and followed the soldiers to the palace. The Guard informed the Sultan, but he took no notice and ordered the Executioner to cut off Aladdin's head. When the people saw that the execution was about to take place, they barricaded the gates and sent a message to the Sultan: if Aladdin was harmed in any way, they would raze the palace to the ground and kill everyone inside.

The Sultan could see the townsfolk swarming over the palace walls so he relented and gave orders for Aladdin to be released and pardoned.

Aladdin went straight to the Sultan, who was seated on his throne, and begged to be told his offence.

"Look out of that window," replied the Sultan, and Aladdin saw the open plain and the level ground where only yesterday his pavilion had stood. "I have pardoned you only so that you may find my daughter. Do not return without her, or I shall not fail to have your head cut off."

For two days, Aladdin wandered about the city, not knowing how to set about finding his wife. He had quite forgotten all the smells and sounds of the bustling streets that were so familiar to him as a child. A friendly shopkeeper who had known his mother gave him a mat to sleep on. When the tap-tapping of the brass workers ceased and the bazaar fell silent, he remembered the sound of the fountain playing outside their pavilion. Without his wife between his arms, sleep would not come to him.

Next morning, he stumbled out of the town in despair and stopped by a river. As he sat by the water and considered whether to drown himself, he wrung his hands and by chance rubbed the magic ring, which he had quite forgotten about.

In a flash, the Genie of the Ring reared up in front of him.

"You have summoned me, Master. What is your wish?"

Aladdin was overjoyed to see the Genie.

"Genie, I want you to return my palace and my wife to me."

"My Lord, I would not even attempt such a thing. This would depend on the Genie of the Lamp who is greater than I."

"Will you at least take me to my palace, wherever it is."

"To hear is to obey." In the bat of an eyelid, Aladdin was spirited away to distant Morocco and set down outside the walls of the pavilion he knew so well. It was now night-time and Aladdin crept under a tree and slept soundly until he was woken by birdsong and the unfamiliar sounds of a foreign town coming to life.

When Zuleika threw open the shutters, she saw her master sitting down below and cried out, "My Lady, my Lady, my Lord Aladdin is seated at the foot of the wall."

The Princess rushed to the window and told Aladdin that it was safe to come up to her room by the private staircase. They kissed and embraced and wept for joy. Aladdin asked his love if she knew where his old lamp was and the full story came out. She told him how the Magician wooed her constantly, telling her that Aladdin's head had been cut off by the Sultan, her father. As for the lamp, she said she knew he always carried it about his person, not putting it down even for a moment.

Aladdin was pleased to discover this and told her his plan.

"I shall go now and return in disguise. Tell Zuleika to watch for me and to let me into the private staircase when she sees me below. Trust me, my beloved," and he went out by the way he had come.

Some time later, Aladdin, dressed as a peasant, found his way to the perfume bazaar, where he bought a powerful potion. He went straight back to the pavilion, where Zuleika let him into the private staircase that led to his wife's apartment.

"Listen carefully, my dearest. I want you to dress in your prettiest robes and invite the Magician to dine with you. Ask for some good red wine and, when he is relaxed and carefree, slip these drops into his wine cup. As soon as he takes the first sip, he will fall down unconscious as if dead."

When the evil Magician came home, he was amazed to see that the Princess had dressed up in her fine clothes and to find that she had stopped mourning her lost husband. She asked if they could

They embraced and wept for joy

sup together that evening, and moreover she had a mind to try the wine of his country, which she had been told was so much better than the wine in Cathay.

After supper, when the Magician's eyes had begun to swim from the wine, the Princess said, "Now that supper is finished, we must do as is the custom in my country. We fill our cups with wine, then each takes the other's cup and quaffs it until it is empty. Here is mine, beloved, and give me yours."

They drank the cups dry and the Magician fell to the floor as if he had been struck dead. The Princess told Zuleika to make the agreed signal to Aladdin. He rushed up, pausing for a second to gaze at the prostrate form of Ebenezer. He threw his arms round his wife and kissed her. Then he told her to leave the room and to take all her handmaidens with her. She was reluctant to let him out of her sight, but she obeyed and, when the door was shut, Aladdin slipped his hand into the Magician's breast pocket. Yes, the lamp was there. He withdrew it. Then he took out his sword and cut off the man's head with a single blow.

Aladdin rubbed the lamp.

"I am the Genie of the Lamp. What is your wish, Master?"

Aladdin told the Genie that he wanted his pavilion with all the people in it taken back to the grounds of the Sultan in Cathay.

Since the loss of his daughter, the Sultan had been inconsolable. Each morning, he threw open the shutters of his bedchamber and looked at the empty space before him until his eyes filled with tears and he could see no more. But on this morning, he threw open the shutters and saw something strange in front of him. "It must be a mirage," he said out loud. He shut his eyes, rubbed them hard and opened them slowly. There was his daughter's pavilion.

"Quickly now," shouted the Sultan. "Fetch my clothes and have my horse saddled." He galloped over to his daughter's pavilion as the Princess and Aladdin came down to meet him. The young couple told their father all that had happened.

The Sultan ordered a public holiday and the whole city celebrated the return of the royal pair. In the streets rose the aromas of roasting goats and oxen, a gift to the townsfolk from the Sultan; music filled the air and, when the Muezzins called the people to prayer, everyone thanked Allah for the happy outcome.

The Tale of the
BIRDS, the BEASTS
and the
CARPENTER

A long time ago, a peacock lived with his peahen by the seashore. At night, they perched safely in the trees, but during the day, they went foraging for food in the forest, where there was an abundance of wild beasts, even lions. They became ever more anxious, so one day they set out together to find somewhere safer to live. After searching for some time, they flew to an island with trees and streams and plenty to eat, where there were no frightening beasts.

Hardly had they settled down, when a duck arrived in a state of great terror and landed beneath the tree on which they were perching. When the Duck had calmed down, the Peacock asked him to tell them what had frightened him.

"I am absolutely sick with sorrow and terrified out of my wits by having met the son of Adam," said the Duck. "I fear for my life every minute of the day."

The Peahen flew down to the Duck and said, "You are welcome to stay with us and no harm shall come to you. Tell us what happened."

The Duck's Tale

I have lived all my life peacefully and safely on this island, but one night I saw in a dream the son of Adam, who spoke with me. Then I heard a voice saying, "Do not trust the son of Adam and do not listen to him. He is crafty with words and as sly as a fox. He nets the fish in the sea, he shoots the birds with pellets of clay, and he even traps the elephant. Nothing escapes him."

I was so alarmed by this dream that from then on, I never had a moment's peace. I went looking for a safe place to live, up towards that mountain over there and, when I reached it, I met a young lion in front of his cave. He was very pleased to see me and asked me my name and what kind of animal I was.

"My name is Duck," I replied, "and I am of the bird family. But tell me, why are you all alone here?"

"My father," said the young Lion, "has always warned me against the son of Adam, and last night I thought I heard a voice warning me in a dream, so I have set out to find this son of Adam and kill him." The young Lion lashed his flanks with his tail at the thought of it.

"O Lion," I said, "I too had a dream warning me to beware the son of Adam but, unlike me, you are strong enough to kill him, so let me go with you."

The young Lion agreed and we set off together. By and by, we saw a dust cloud in the distance and, when we reached it, we found a strange creature rolling in the dust.

"What is your name, creature, and what are you doing?" asked the young Lion.

The creature replied, "O King of the Wild Beasts, I am Ass and

I saw in a dream the son of Adam

I have just escaped from the son of Adam, who tied a packsaddle on my back, which was held by a tight girth round my belly and a crupper under my tail, and in my mouth he placed a metal bit. If I fell down or stumbled with tiredness, he struck me with a goad and when I brayed, he cursed me. If I had not escaped, I would have had to live like this until I was too slow for him and then I would have been sold to the water carriers and had to carry even heavier burdens until I dropped dead. My poor carcass would be thrown on a dungheap and eaten by dogs. This is why I ran away at dawn. When you came upon me, I was rolling in the dirt to relieve the pain in my back. But mark my words, the son of Adam has already set out to catch me."

Just then, we saw another cloud of dust nearby and the Ass brayed with fear, breaking wind loudly. Out of the dust cloud appeared a magnificent black-coated beast, a white blaze on its forehead and white markings above its hooves.

"And what kind of animal are you, majestic creature? And why do you flee across the desert?" asked the young Lion when the beast stopped in front of us.

"O King of the Wild Beasts," replied the creature, "I am Horse and I am fleeing the son of Adam."

"But how is this possible?" cried the young Lion. "Though I'm not yet full grown, I was searching for the son of Adam in order to kill him and calm the fears of this poor duck. Now I find that you too, a magnificent tall creature strong enough to kill the son of Adam with one blow from a hoof, are afraid of him."

The Horse laughed when he heard this and said, "You cannot imagine how clever and cunning is the son of Adam. He hobbles my four feet, places a saddle on my back held with two girths, puts an iron bit in my mouth and attaches reins on either side. He prods my flanks with metal stirrups until they bleed. When I grow old and cannot go fast enough for him, he will sell me to the Miller. I will have to turn the millstone day after day until I drop dead. Then my carcass will be sold to the Knacker, who will flay my hide, render my flesh to make candles and pluck out my tail to sell to the Sieve Maker. I ran away from the son of Adam at midday but I know he is on my trail."

At that moment, we all looked with alarm towards another cloud of dust, but when it settled, a furious creature appeared in front of us, gurgling and pawing the ground. The young Lion thought this must be the son of Adam and was just about to spring at him when I said, "O Lion, this is not the son of Adam."

"Who are you, and from whom are you fleeing?" asked the Lion.

"I am Camel," replied the creature without stopping his gurgling and pawing, "and I am fleeing from the son of Adam."

"How is this possible," asked the Lion, "seeing what a large creature you are? You could crush anyone with your weight."

"O King of the Wild Beasts, did you but know how crafty and powerful the son of Adam is. No one can defeat him, save only Death. He puts twine of goat's hair through my nostrils to make a ring, so that the smallest child can lead me. He loads me with the heaviest burdens and makes me go on long journeys across the desert. When I am old, he doesn't keep me: he sells me to the Knacker, who cuts my throat, sells my hide to the tanners and my flesh to the cooks. I ran away at sundown and he is after me this very hour. Let me go, so that I can flee to the safety of the wilds."

"Wait awhile," said the young Lion, lashing his flanks with his tail. "You can watch me tear the son of Adam apart. I will give you his flesh to eat, while I drink his blood and crunch up his bones." But the Ass, the Horse and the Camel were too fearful to stay, so they went on their way with all possible speed.

Now at that moment we saw yet another cloud of dust in the distance and when it drew near, there appeared a creature, slight of stature and lean limbed, a bag of carpenter's tools on its shoulder and eight planks of wood balanced on its head. I was rooted to the ground with fear as I watched the young Lion approach the creature, who smiled and said in a respectful voice, "Greetings, O King of the Wild Beasts. I am in sore need of your protection for only you are strong enough to save me."

"Certainly I shall protect you, but first tell me what sort of a wild beast you are, for I have never met anyone so fine-looking as you, and with such eloquence of speech."

"I am Carpenter, O King, and I am fleeing from the son of Adam who follows me and will be upon us by dawn."

The young Lion seethed with fury and let out a mighty roar.

"I shall keep guard tonight and kill this son of Adam when I meet him," he said. "But tell me, where are you going with this bag and these planks of wood?"

"I am on the way to your father's Wazir, the Lynx," replied the Carpenter, "to make him a dwelling that will protect him from the son of Adam."

You are in a trap, stupid beast

"Then you must first build me one, before you go on your way," growled the young Lion.

"I cannot do that until I have finished the dwelling for the Wazir, but I shall return," said the Carpenter.

Seeing how slight and feeble the Carpenter appeared, the young Lion roared, "No, first you will build one for me," and to drive home his command, he gave the Carpenter a blow with his paw that sent him sprawling and dazed to the ground.

When the Carpenter recovered, he rose to his feet, but concealed his fury. "Well then, I will build you a dwelling first," he said with a smile and, using his planks, he made a box that was open at one end. Close by lay the door, the nails to secure it and a hammer. "Now you must try it for size, O King."

The young Lion crouched down and scrambled into the box so that only his tail was outside.

"Be patient: I'll see if there is room for your tail," said the Carpenter and, taking up the young Lion's tail, he twisted it into a ball and pushed it in. He grabbed the door, placed it on the end of the box and drove home the nails. Then he stood back and laughed.

"What is this narrow house that you have made for me, Carpenter? Let me out."

"You are in a trap, stupid beast, and there is no escape for you," replied the Carpenter.

I knew then that this was the son of Adam of whom I had dreamt, and that my protector had been trapped by his greater cunning.

The young Lion knew also that this was the son of Adam, of whom he had been warned by his father, as well as by the voice in his dream. For him it was too late but I crept slowly away. When I looked back, I saw the Carpenter dig a deep pit, push the box into it, pile bits of wood on top and set it alight. I have been two days fleeing to this place and now I even fear my own shadow.

After the Duck had finished his story, the Peacock and the Peahen were silent for a while. Then the Peacock spread his tail in defiance and cried his piercing cry.

"See?" said the Peahen. "You are safe here, for we shall protect you." But the Duck did not believe her.

The Tale of
SINBAD
the
SAILOR

In Baghdad, there was once a poor man called Sinbad who earned his living as a porter, carrying goods from place to place. One hot day, he had carried such a heavy load that he felt his knees begin to give way. Seeing a bench in front of the garden wall of a house, he sat down to recover.

From an open window Sinbad heard pleasant sounds of talk and laughter. He got up and peered through the gate. The piping of flutes and sweet singing delighted his ears; the smell of sizzling meats, his nostrils. His eyes took in the beautiful garden, filled with fragrant flowers and shady trees, criss-crossed by servants bearing succulent dishes. He felt quite dizzy with hunger, so he sat down on the bench again and sang a song praising Allah for the rewards He doled out to the rich and asking Allah to forgive his sins – for he must have sinned greatly in his life to be so poor compared to someone like this, who lived like a king.

Sinbad was about to shoulder his load and go on his way when a young page came out of the gate, saying that his Master had heard his song and wished to invite him in.

Sinbad was led into a room where the host sat at a table feasting with his richly attired friends.

"Come sit by me," said the host in a kindly voice, "but first, tell us your name and calling."

"My name is Sinbad and I make my living as a porter."

His host smiled and said, "And I, my friend, am Sinbad the Sailor. Be doubly welcome and, while you eat, I shall tell you my story and show you how I came by these riches."

The Tale of the First Voyage

My father, who was a merchant in Baghdad, died when I was still a child, leaving me well set up. As soon as I was of age, I began to squander my fortune in riotous living until only my house and some goods remained. I saw how foolish I had been and decided to make a new life before I lost everything. I sold what was left, bought merchandise suitable for trading and embarked from Basra with a company of other merchants on a ship that sailed from isle to isle.

One day, we anchored off an island that seemed like a corner of paradise with all its luxuriant vegetation and sweet birdsong. We went ashore and, while some bathed or lit fires for cooking, others including myself went exploring. After a while, I lay down to rest and fell asleep.

I was woken by the distant cries of the Captain urging everyone to return to the vessel as fast as they could, for it was not an island on which we had come ashore, but a huge sea creature! It had been

For a day, a night and yet another day, I floated astride the barrel

asleep for so long that trees had grown on its back and birds had come to live there. The fires of my companions had woken the monster and at any moment we would surely be flung into the sea and drowned. Some people reached the ship in time, but I did not and suddenly the waves closed over me. I struggled to reach the surface, but was lucky to catch hold of a floating barrel that must have been left behind by my companions. I clung to it, feeling helpless, as I watched my ship disappear over the horizon.

For a day, a night and yet another day, I floated astride the barrel, until the winds drove me to an island, where I pulled myself ashore. My legs were numb and I could see where fish had nibbled at my feet. I fell down in a swoon and slept until the next day, by which time my feet were so swollen and painful that I could only crawl.

After a few days, thanks to the plentiful fruit I found to eat, I recovered my strength and set off to explore the island. As I was walking on the shore, I was amazed to see a fine-looking horse tethered to a rock. A man appeared from behind the rocks and came towards me. He explained that he was one of King Mihrjan's grooms.

"Every month, at the time of the new moon, we grooms take the King's mares to the shore, where we tether them close to the water. Then we hide and at full tide the sea-stallions scent the mares and come out of the water to mate. In this way, the King's mares breed the best foals in the world. Come, I shall take you to the King."

The King treated me with great courtesy, gave me clothes to wear and a house to live in. He eventually made me the Clerk of the Port and Registrar of all the boats that used it.

After some time had passed, a ship with many merchants aboard came into port. When all the goods I could see had been marked off, I asked the Captain if anything else remained in the hold.

"Yes," he replied, "but only some merchandise belonging to a passenger who drowned trying to escape a huge sea monster. I plan to return the goods to his family in Baghdad. His name was Sinbad."

"Captain," said I, "I am that man. I am Sinbad."

I reminded him of conversations between us until he believed me and gave me my bales of merchandise. I checked them and nothing was missing. I presented the most precious items to the King and asked him if I could return with the ship to my own country. He was sad to let me go but agreed, after first loading me with precious gifts. When I reached home, my family welcomed me and I was able to live a life of luxury again.

Now, my friend, you have cheered us up with your company today, so come and dine again tomorrow.

In the morning, Sinbad the Porter washed and dressed in his best clothes and returned to Sinbad the Sailor's house. Though there were many guests, when they sat down to eat, he was again seated next to their host. After they had eaten, Sinbad the Sailor began the tale of his second adventure.

The Tale of the Second Voyage

I lived for some time without a care in the world, but eventually I grew bored and decided to undertake another voyage. I went downriver to Basra, found a fine new ship and set sail with fellow merchants, trading wherever the ship called.

Trade prospered as before. We merchants were contented and, when, by chance, we passed a verdant island, the Captain decided to anchor and let us go ashore. We found a little paradise, where shady trees bore delicious fruit and streams of crystal water ran down to the shore. I lay down in a quiet spot and fell asleep.

Sinbad found a fine new ship and set sail

Imagine my dismay when I awoke to find that the ship had sailed without me! I waited some time but the ship did not return. After cursing my stupidity for ever having set off on another voyage, I went to look for help, but there was not a living being on the whole island and I almost went out of my mind with misery.

In desperation, I climbed a high tree and saw a strange white object on the horizon. I scrambled down and made my way towards it. I could not fathom it at all: huge, white and with a smooth surface. It took me fifty paces to walk round it, but as I reached my starting point, I was suddenly plunged in darkness. I looked up, and a bird so large that it filled the sky was about to land on top of me. I fled into the undergrowth and, as I did so, I remembered travellers' tales of the mighty Rukh bird, which was strong enough to carry off an elephant in its claws. This white object was none other than the Rukh bird's egg, on which it now settled and fell asleep.

Here was my chance to escape. I took off my turban and twisted it into a strong rope while I crept round behind the bird. I tied myself to one of its legs and waited until dawn. The Rukh stood up, stretched its wings and, with a deafening flapping, took off, climbing higher and higher into the sky until I felt quite dizzy. At last, it alighted on a hilltop where I was able to unbind myself and escape amongst the trees.

When I emerged

into a valley, I saw that I was surrounded by mountains whose summits pierced the sky. I regretted that I had left the island, for was I not worse off now?

However, I took courage and followed the path of a stream, hoping it would lead me to the sea. Soon I noticed that the ground glistened and sparkled all round me and, when I bent down, I found it was the sun reflecting in diamonds. They were everywhere, like pebbles on a beach. But my excitement was soon dashed by finding myself surrounded by vipers and snakes that were as thick as the branch of a tree.

I staggered along, giddy with fear, when all of a sudden I just missed being flattened by a sheep's flayed carcass, which fell from the sky. Then I remembered an ancient tale of merchants who threw carcasses from a mountain top into a valley where diamonds lay thick on the ground, but where it was too dangerous to go because of the venomous snakes. The diamonds became embedded in the soft flesh of the carcasses. Eagles picked up the carcasses and carried them back to their eyries on the mountain tops, where the merchants were waiting for the birds' return. They drove the birds off and collected the sparkling gems.

When I remembered this tale, I filled my pockets with diamonds and attached myself with my turban to the underside of the carcass. Moments later, a mighty eagle swooped down upon it, grasped it in its claws, with me clinging underneath, and flew up to his mountain eyrie. As he landed, a man rushed up, shouting and waving a stout stick. The eagle flew off, but when the man saw me appear from underneath the carcass, he was rooted to the ground in terror. I did my best to calm him and when his fellow merchants appeared, I shared with them some of the gems that I had collected in my pockets. They took me with them over the mountains to a fair country and, with the diamonds that I had kept, I was able to buy more merchandise. By slow degrees, I made my way back to Baghdad, richer than when I had left.

Tomorrow, come and dine with me again and I shall tell you more.

Sinbad the Porter returned for another five nights until Sinbad the Sailor had told him of all his remaining voyages and how each time he returned he was richer than when he had left. He told how on the third voyage he and his crew had been blown off course towards an island from which no one had ever returned. There they escaped from a giant who ate the ship's master. The giant would have eaten them all had they not blinded him in his sleep with a burning branch.

Sinbad told his namesake how during his fourth voyage he was shipwrecked and cast ashore with his fellow mariners. They were captured by cannibals who fattened them up for a feast. But Sinbad starved himself so that he was not worth eating, and he was spared. He escaped and met up with another tribe, whom he taught to make saddles for their horses. In return, he was given a wife and jewels.

It was the custom of these people to bury a man alive with his wife, should the wife die before him. She did, and he was duly left to die from starvation in the burial chamber. Again he managed to escape alive. He bartered the jewels as he made his way back to Basra and, once more, arrived richer than when he had left.

A mighty eagle grasped the carcass in its claws

On the fifth voyage, his vessel anchored off an island where the sailors found a giant Rukh's nest with an enormous egg. This they stole and broke open. Inside was a huge chick just about to hatch. They killed it and carved themselves delicious steaks. When the parents returned and found their chick eaten, they picked up great rocks with their mighty talons and dropped them on to the fleeing vessel so that it sank. By clinging to a plank, Sinbad safely reached the shore. There he met an old man who asked for help in crossing a stream. He hoisted the man on to his shoulders but, when they had crossed, the old man refused to let go.

For days and nights his life was a torment of beatings and labour. He only escaped by fermenting some grapes and making the old man so drunk that he fell into a deep sleep. His next encounter was with a tribe who collected valuable coconuts and sold them in nearby towns. Sinbad made a fortune by exchanging them for pearls – not prized by the natives but of great value when he returned home.

On the sixth voyage, his ship was blown on to a mountainous headland where a thousand wrecks and their cargo littered the beach. Coming across a river that plunged into a cliff face, he built a raft and loaded it with treasure from the wrecks. Then he launched himself on the torrent and was swept down through the mountains to the land of Sarandib. He presented his booty to the King who gave him rich gifts for the Kalifeh of Baghdad in exchange.

The homeward voyage was to be his last, but the Kalifeh insisted he return with gifts for the mighty King of Sarandib. On the way, Sinbad was enslaved by an ivory trader who forced him to hunt and kill elephants. Only when the elephants showed him their ancient burial ground and the mountains of tusks there for the taking, did his captor allow him to return to Baghdad, a rich man again.

When Sinbad the Sailor had recounted this seventh and final voyage, he said to Sinbad the Porter, "Now, my friend, you have heard of the labours and hardships that I have undergone. Would you not say that your life as a porter, poor as you are, has been more tranquil than mine as a voyager? But come, I have enjoyed your company so much that I invite you to live in my house, to be my companion and share my good fortune. As I am known as Sinbad the Sailor, you shall be called Sinbad the Landsman."

And so they both lived happily until they were gathered in death by Allah, the Lord of the seas and the land.

The Tale of the

FOX

and the

COCK

In a village there lived a man who kept a goodly number of chickens. Amongst them, there was an old Cock, who had enjoyed many near escapes in his long life and so had become both wise and wary. However, he was also a little forgetful and, one day, after wandering about the fields and hedgerows and finding all manner of good things to eat, he saw that the evening was drawing in and that he was not quite sure of the direction of his home.

Just as he was casting about for a familiar landmark, he caught sight of a fox, still at some distance but getting closer by the second. Luckily, there was a high wall nearby so, to avoid danger, he spread his wings, took to the air and flew up on to the coping.

When the Fox arrived at the foot of the wall, he saw the Cock and called up to him with a friendly greeting. The Cock ignored him and pretended not to hear.

The Fox called again and told him off for his lack of manners. Still the Cock made no reply, his eyes fixed unblinking on the

The old Cock inclined his head towards the Fox

distance, where he could now see the direction of his home.

"Listen to me," cried the Fox, "for I have been sent as an envoy by Lion, the King of the Beasts, and Eagle, the King of the Birds. They have found a beautiful meadow on the banks of a sweetly flowing brook. There they have assembled all manner of beasts and birds to celebrate peace, brotherhood and love amongst us all. There are hyenas, lynxes and leopards, gazelles and antelopes. From the birds, I have already seen vultures, ravens, turtledoves and quail. They are all feeding and grazing happily and are at peace with one another. I have been sent out to spread the good news and to bring any other animal I come across to the meeting."

The old Cock still pretended not to hear a word, but looked straight ahead towards his home in the distance.

The Fox scolded the Cock for his ill-mannered behaviour and asked what reply he should bring to the Kings of the Beasts and the Birds, for he warned that they would punish anyone severely who did not obey the summons.

The old Cock inclined his head towards the Fox. "Brother," he said, "I had just made my mind up to come with you when I spotted something in the distance which has filled me with dread."

"And what is that, Brother?" asked the Fox.

"I see a dust cloud approaching and falcons circling above. I am so afraid, Brother. What shall we do?"

The Fox enquired nervously if the Cock could see anything resembling a greyhound.

"Well," replied the Cock, "now that you mention it, I can see animals with long, lean bodies, powerful limbs and laid-back ears that are racing towards us."

"In that case," replied the Fox, "I must be off."

"But, Brother," called out the Cock as the Fox turned to leave, "I thought you had been sent to invite every beast and bird to this gathering of peace and love."

"Indeed I was, Brother," said the Fox, as he took to his heels, "but now that I come to think of it, the Greyhound was not mentioned and I am no friend of his."

As soon as the Fox was out of sight, the Cock flew down from the wall and ran home as fast as his legs could carry him, praising Allah for delivering him from mortal danger.

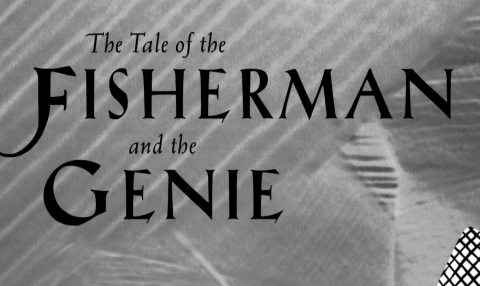

The Tale of the
FISHERMAN
and the
GENIE

here was once a poor fisherman who had a wife and three children. It was his custom to cast his net four times a day and no more. One day he went down to the seashore, cast his net, waited until it settled, gathered the lines and tried to haul it in. It was far too heavy, so he carried the ends ashore, tied them to a stake and was just able to heave the net in, only to find that it contained a dead donkey.

"What sort of a living can I make with a dead donkey?" he cried.

The Fisherman freed the dead donkey from the net, waded out into the sea and cast the net again. He found it heavier than the first time and, believing there were fish inside, he hauled it up on to dry land. What did he find but a large earthen pitcher full of sand and mud. He cleaned his net and returned to the sea to cast it again. When he pulled it in, he found only cracked pots and broken glass. Raising his eyes to heaven, he said, "Allah! Thou knowest that I only cast my net four times in a day and this is the fourth time. Pray let me catch enough for my daily bread."

He cast his net and waited for it to settle, but he had to haul with all his might to land it. This time, he found a huge brass bottle. The mouth of the bottle was stopped with a lead cap, stamped with the seal of King Solomon.

The Fisherman rejoiced and said, "If I sell it in the brass bazaar, this jar is worth ten golden dinars, but first I must find out what is inside." He cut the lead seal with his knife and eased the stopper from the bottle, but he found nothing in it. All the more was his astonishment when he saw a stream of vapour that began to pour from the jar and spiral heavenwards. Once it had reached its full height, the pillar of vapour condensed and became a genie – a gigantic figure, the crown of whose head touched the clouds, though his feet were on the ground.

When the Fisherman saw the Genie, his teeth chattered and his mouth dried up. The Genie looked at him and cried, "There is no God but Allah and King Solomon is His prophet. I swear on pain of death never again to sin against Him."

"O mighty Genie," responded the Fisherman, "did you say King Solomon? But he has been dead some one thousand and eight hundred years."

When the evil spirit heard these words, he said, "Well, Fisherman, you must die this very hour."

"Why should I die?" cried the Fisherman. "What have I done to deserve death, I who freed you from the bottle and saved you from the depths of the sea? What is my crime?"

"The only choice I allow you," answered the Genie, "is the manner of your death. Meanwhile, listen to my story and you will learn why you must die. I am one of the rebel genies that sinned against King Solomon. He sent his wazir to seize me and I was

The pillar of vapour condensed and became a genie

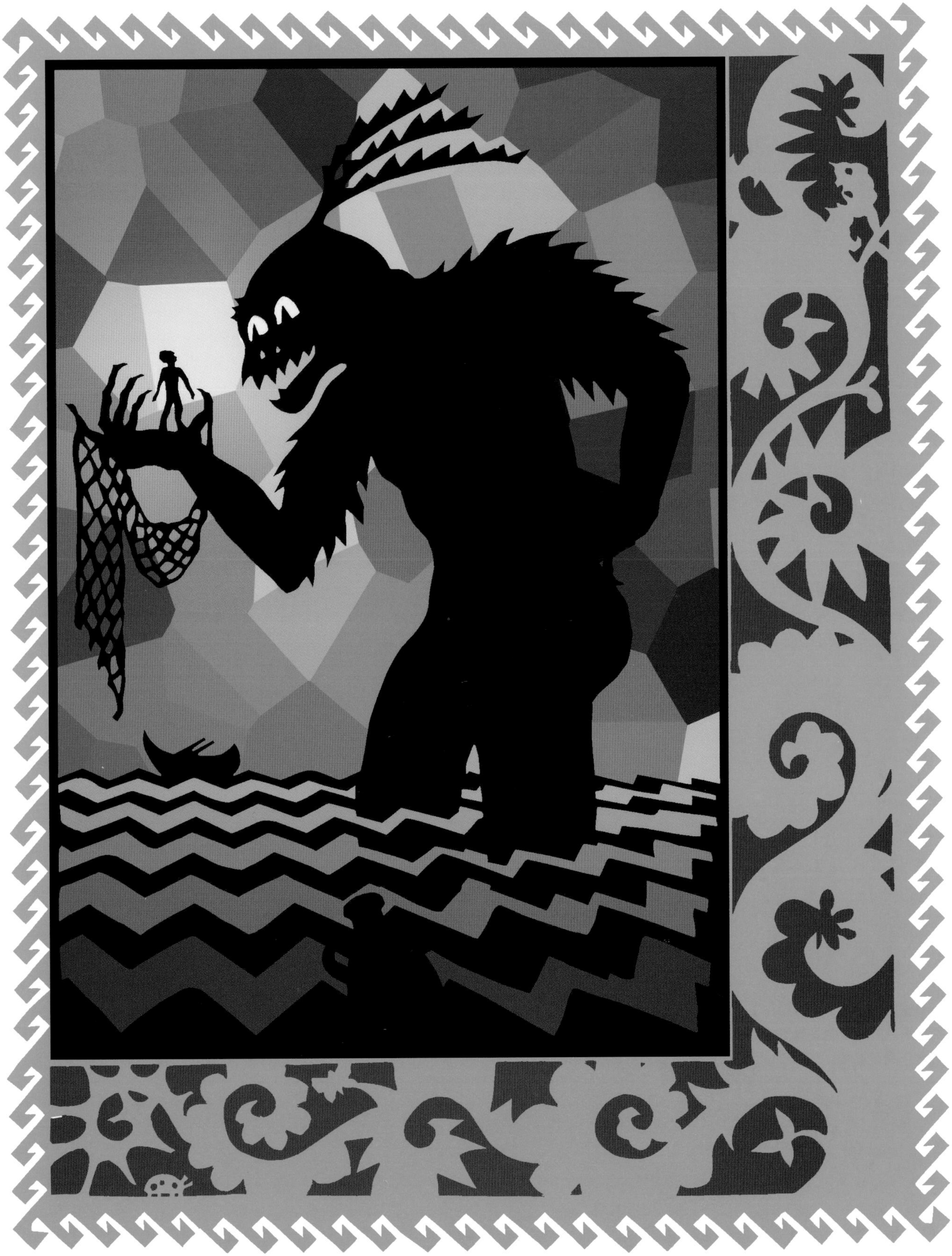

brought in chains to stand before him as if I were a common thief. When King Solomon saw me, he ordered me to embrace his own faith. I refused, so he sent for this bottle, shut me inside, stopped it with lead that was stamped with his legendary seal and ordered his servant to carry it down to the sea and cast it into the waves.

"There I stayed for a hundred years. In my heart, I promised that anyone who released me I would make rich for life. When a hundred years had passed without being released, I promised that whoever did so would be rewarded with any treasure on earth. Still no one set me free so I promised that I would offer my rescuer three wishes. After waiting yet another hundred years I became furious and swore to myself, now I will kill the man who releases me, but I will let him choose how to die."

When the poor Fisherman heard this, he said, "Spare my life, Genie, in case Allah sends someone to kill you."

But the Genie only repeated, "I promised to kill the person who set me free. Choose how you wish to die."

"So the old saying is true," said the Fisherman, "a good deed doesn't succeed."

The Genie was becoming impatient but the Fisherman had not given up hope. "This is only a genie," he said to himself. "No matter how powerful he is, I am a man and should be able to outwit him."

"In the name of Allah," he called out to the Genie, "will you allow me one question before I die? And will you promise to give me a truthful answer?"

"I will, but be quick," said the Genie, who was a little disturbed by the mention of the holy name of Allah.

"Tell me then, Genie, how did you fit into this bottle, when it couldn't even contain one of your toes?"

"Are you saying you don't believe me?" shouted the Genie furiously.

"No, I don't," said the Fisherman, "though I would if I could see it with my own eyes."

Straight away, the Genie began to change into a wreath of vapour and slid slowly into the bottle. The Fisherman waited till he was inside and banged on the lead stopper.

"Now, Genie, it is your turn to choose how you want to die. I shall fling you into the sea where you have lived for many hundreds of years, and now you will be there till the day of judgement. I told you Allah would spare you if you spared me, but you would not listen and now Allah has delivered you into my hands." The Fisherman took the bottle and set off for the water's edge, while the Genie called out to him most pitiably.

"Spare me, good Fisherman. Be as generous to me as I have been wicked to you. Set me free, I beg you, and I vow I shall never do you harm. Indeed, I will help you to achieve great wealth."

So, in the end, the Fisherman relented and, after making the Genie swear to keep to his promise, he removed the stopper. Out flew the vapour, which transformed itself back into the hideous Genie who straight away kicked the bottle far out into the sea.

The Fisherman piddled in his pants, he was so frightened. "This does not bode well," he told himself, but he took courage and said, "Remember your promise, Genie. If you reward kindness with wickedness, Allah will punish you."

"Follow me, Fisherman," replied the Genie simply, and he set off through the city, beyond the walls, into the wild uplands and down into a desert surrounded by four mountains. In the middle of the desert stood a lake and here the Genie stopped and told the Fisherman to cast his net.

The Fisherman was astonished to see fish of four different colours: white, red, blue and yellow. He quickly cast his net and caught one of each colour.

"Now, take these fish," ordered the Genie, "and place them before the Sultan. He will make you a wealthy man."

With that, the Genie said a hasty farewell and struck the ground with his foot. It opened beneath him and he was swallowed up.

The Fisherman took the fish and made for the city. He went to the Sultan's palace and laid the fish before him. The Sultan was filled with wonder at the sight, for never in his life had he seen such fish. He gave the Fisherman four hundred gold dinars and asked his Wazir to take the fishes to the Cook.

The Cook cleaned them and set them in the frying pan until one side was evenly cooked. Then she turned them over and at that instant the fish raised their heads from the pan and cried out most mournfully, "Come back, come back and set us free."

At this, the kitchen wall split asunder and out came a beautiful young woman, her eyelids darkened with black kohl, her silk robe fringed with blue tassels and wearing rings of priceless jewels on her fingers. In one hand she carried a wand that she thrust into the frying pan and overturned it. With that, she disappeared the way she had come and the wall closed behind her. When the Wazir came for the fish, the tearful Cook told him what had happened.

The fish cried out, "Come back, come back and set us free."

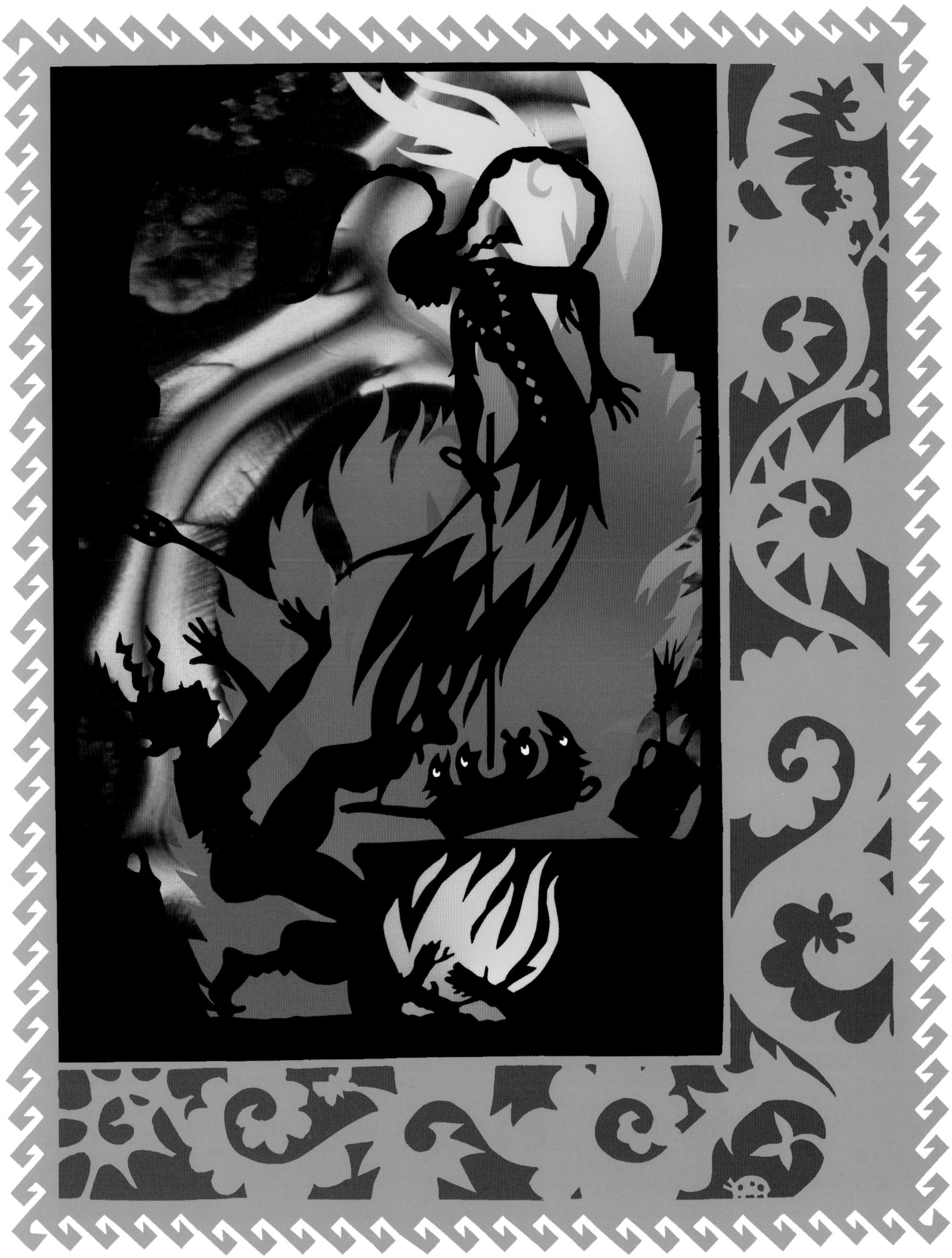

"This is a very strange story you tell," said the Wazir. He sent for the Fisherman and asked him to bring four fish exactly as before.

The Fisherman returned to the lake, cast his net and caught four fish: white, red, blue and yellow. He carried these to the Wazir who took them to the Cook. "Fry these before my eyes," he said, "so that I may see what you do."

So the Cook cleaned the fish, and set them in the frying pan over the fire. As they began to sizzle, the fish lifted their heads and repeated, "Come back, come back and set us free."

At this, the beautiful girl burst through the wall, overturned the pan as before and disappeared. The Wazir cried out, "What can it mean? Certainly we must not hide this from the Sultan." And off he went to tell him what had happened.

"Why, I must see this with my own eyes," said the Sultan and sent for the Fisherman to bring four more fish like the others. The Fisherman soon brought the fish and once again the Sultan gave him four hundred gold dinars.

The Sultan turned to the Wazir and said, "Fry me the fish while I watch you," so the Wazir sent for the frying pan, threw the cleaned fish into it and put it on the fire.

As had happened before, the fish lifted their heads from the pan with their sorrowful cry: "Come back, come back and set us free." And as before, the pan was overturned and the fish were charred as black as charcoal.

The Sultan was utterly bewildered and he turned to the Wazir. "We can't let this matter rest," he said. "Some strange events are connected with these fish."

He asked the Fisherman where the fish came from. The Fisherman told him about the lake in the desert between the four mountains, just a short walk away and still in sight of the city. The Sultan was deeply puzzled: how could such a place exist in his own Kingdom? He summoned his horsemen and, guided by the Fisherman – who went ahead, cursing the Genie in his mind – they climbed a mountain and came down into a desert that they had never seen before. He was amazed to find this wilderness set amid four mountains, with the lake and its fish of four colours, and was rooted to the spot in wonderment.

He asked his horsemen, "Has any of you ever seen or heard tell of this stretch of water?"

All replied, "Never in all our days, O Sultan."

"By Allah, I will not return to my throne until I learn the truth about this lake and these fish."

He ordered his men to pitch camp by the lake and summoned his Wazir, telling him, "I shall set out alone tonight on foot to discover the source of these mysteries."

The Sultan changed his clothes, slung his sword over his shoulder and took a path up one of the mountains. He marched for two days and two nights until he spotted a dark building in the far distance.

When he drew near, he found it was a palace built of black stone, reinforced with ironwork. One side of the gate was wide open, the other shut. The Sultan's spirits rose as he stood before the gate and rapped on it lightly. Then he knocked as loudly as he could but still there was no answer, so he went through the gate and into a great hall crying, "I am a stranger and a wayfarer." Still no reply.

He passed through the hall into the heart of the palace. It was richly furnished with silk rugs starred with gold. In the middle was a spacious court, off which were four sitting rooms facing one another. A canopy shaded the court and in the centre was a fountain with four lions of red gold, spouting water as clear as crystal from their mouths. Birds flew in the air beneath a net of golden wire. In brief, there was everything except a living person.

The Sultan felt sad for he found no one to ask about the mystery of the lake, the fish, the mountains and the palace. As he sat down to rest, he heard a mournful voice saying, "O Fate, see this poor prisoner. Show mercy to one who has fallen into this sad state. Let me escape, I pray."

When the Sultan heard these words he sprang to his feet and followed the sound to a curtained doorway. He parted the curtain

The Sultan's spirits rose as he stood before the gate

and saw a young man sitting on a couch: a fair youth, his forehead pale as parchment. The Sultan saluted the youth, but the young man remained seated in his silk robe shot with Egyptian gold and his crown studded with gems, sorrow written on his fair face. He said, "O my lord, I should rise to greet you but I must beg your pardon, for I cannot do so." He lifted the skirt of his robe, showing that his lower half, from his navel to his toes, was made of stone, while from his navel to the crown of his head he was a man.

The Sultan cried out, "Young man, you heap sorrow on sorrow. I came to solve the mystery of the fish, but now I need to hear your story. Lose no time, but tell me the whole tale."

The youth began, "My story, and that of the fish, is a strange one and will be a dire warning to anyone hearing it."

"Tell me," said the Sultan.

The Spellbound Prince's Tale

My father, Mahmud, Lord of the Black Isles and what is now these four mountains, was Sultan of this city. He ruled for three score years and ten, after which the Lord took him and I reigned as Sultan. I married my cousin – a beautiful girl and the daughter of my father's brother. She appeared to love me so deeply that whenever I was absent she neither ate nor drank until she saw me again.

Five happy years passed until, one day, she went to bathe at the Hammam and I bade our cook prepare the supper. I lay down on my bed and summoned two damsels to fan me, one at my head and the other at my feet. But I was restless without my wife and could not sleep, for though my eyes were closed, my mind was wide awake.

Presently, I heard the slave girl at my head say to the one at my feet, "How wretched our master is! What a shame it is that his wife betrays him so cruelly!"

"Is our master blind or just stupid?" said the slave girl at my feet. "He never asks her where she goes at night."

"Of course not," replied the girl at my head. "She drugs him every night before she leaves, so how could he know that she goes out perfumed and dressed in her richest raiment? It's only on her return at dawn that she burns a powder under his nose to wake him."

When I heard this, my world turned black. That night we ate and drank together as usual until she called for the wine I usually had before going to bed. I did not drink it but led her to believe that I had fallen into a deep sleep.

She rose and put on her loveliest dress and sweetest perfumes, then she slung my sword over her shoulder, opened the palace gates and went on her wicked way. I arose and followed her, threading through the streets until she came to the city gate, where she spoke words I did not understand. The padlocks fell away like magic and the gate opened. Eventually, she came to the rubbish heaps on the outskirts of the city. She entered a hut made of mud bricks, but I was able to climb on to the roof to see what was happening inside. To my horror, I saw my fair wife greeting a slave.

"What kept you away all this time?" he asked my wife angrily.

"My Lord and apple of my eye, you know that I am married to my cousin whom I loathe from top to toe. If it were not for fear of harming you, I would turn this city to a heap of rubble where ravens croak and owls hoot, jackals prowl and wolves loot."

She begged him to forgive her. When I saw my wife, my own cousin, embrace this ruffian, I almost went mad. I climbed down,

entered the hut, grabbed my sword and struck at the slave. I thought I had killed him but, as I later discovered, I had only wounded him.

Once back at the palace, I lay on my bed and slept until morning.

When my wife awoke me, she blamed me bitterly for wounding the darling of her heart.

"By my magic powers," she screamed, "I make you half man, half stone." And this is how you see me now, unable to rise, neither dead nor alive. But worse was to come. She put a spell on all my Kingdom, turning the four Black Isles into mountains and all my people – the Muslims, the Magi, the Jews and the Christians – into fish of different colours. She tortures me every day, giving me a hundred lashes with a whip.

As he finished his terrible tale, the young man dissolved into tears.

"Where is this woman and the slave?" asked the Sultan.

"They are over there, under the dome of the tomb in the palace gardens. He has spoken not a word, but she feeds him sweetmeats, soup and wine all day and then at sunrise comes to beat me."

"By Allah, I shall avenge you," said the Sultan.

He sat talking to the young Prince until nightfall and then lay down to sleep. He was up before sunrise, drew his sword and entered the tomb where the rare perfumes and the glimmering candles directed him to the wounded slave. With a single blow, the Sultan struck him dead and then quickly hid his body down a well. Dressing in the slave's clothes, he lay down under the dome, his sword concealed at his side. As dawn broke, the wicked wife went to her husband, stripped him of his clothes and flogged him cruelly.

Then she went down to the slave, taking with her a goblet of fine wine and a bowl of broth.

"Speak to me. Say something, beloved," she pleaded. "How long shall I have to suffer like this?"

The Sultan twisted his tongue to disguise his voice and said, "You do not deserve that I speak to you, when you torment your husband so. He keeps me awake night and day with his cries to Heaven. It is this that has prevented me from speaking for so long."

The sorceress almost fainted with joy that at last her love had recovered his power of speech.

"If that is what you want, my beloved, I will go at once and release my loathsome husband from his spell."

She went straight to the palace, where she took a metal bowl, filled it with water and spoke strange words that made the contents bubble and boil though there was no fire to heat it. With this water she sprinkled her husband, saying, "Come forth out of this enchanted form into thy former form."

At this, the young man shook and trembled all over. He rose slowly to his feet.

"Go, and do not return. If you do, I will kill you," the sorceress screamed in his face.

So he went and hid in the palace gardens while she rushed back to where she thought her darling lay, and begged him to rise.

The Sultan, still talking in a low, faint voice, said, "You have rid me of the branch, but not the root of the trouble. Every night, the people of the kingdom whom you have turned into fish raise their heads above the lake and call out and I cannot get well. Set them free and then come and raise me from my sickbed, for I already feel a little strength returning."

At once the witch sprang to her feet. "I shall do your bidding without delay, beloved."

Full of joy, she ran down to the lake, took some water in the palm of her hand and murmured strange words over it. Instantly, the fish of four colours lifted their heads from the lake and, with a cry of joy, turned back into Muslims, Magi, Jews and Christians; the lake again became a crowded city, the bazaars were thronged with people plying their trades and the four mountains changed into the Black Isles, as they had once been.

She ran quickly back to the tomb.

"O my dear love!" she cried eagerly. "Stretch out your hand so that I may help you up."

"Come closer to me," said the Sultan and when she had drawn near enough, he grabbed the sword that lay hidden by his side and struck her. The blade pierced her heart and she fell down dead.

The Sultan left the tomb, found where the young Prince was hiding and told him the news of his Kingdom's happy release from the enchantress's spell.

"Now, young Prince," he said, "will you stay here or come back with me to my city? It's only a short ride away."

"Sultan, your city is a year's journey from mine. It was only because of the spell that you could come here in such a short time. But I will not part from you, even for the winking of an eye."

The Sultan was overjoyed.

"From this day on, you will be my son, for I have never been

The fish turned back into Muslims, Magi, Jews and Christians

blessed with one, and I shall be your father. We shall rule our lands together," he said and they embraced each other.

They journeyed for a full year before they arrived at the Sultan's palace. After setting his Kingdom to rights, the Sultan said to his Wazir, "Now fetch me the Fisherman who brought us the fish."

The Fisherman hurried to the palace and the Sultan said to him, "But for you, I would not have a son, and both he and the people of his kingdom would be under the spell of a wicked enchantress."

He gave the Fisherman the finest clothes and all the riches the man could desire. When the Sultan learnt that the Fisherman had two daughters, he took one for his own wife and the young Prince married the other.

And so they lived in the full joy of life until death took them and the Fisherman became the richest man in the Kingdom.

The Teller of Tales
SHAHRAZADE
The Last Night

When almost three years had run their course, by which time Shahrazade had borne the King three sons, she said to him, "Great King, for a thousand nights and a night, I have told you stories about past times and people who lived before us. Now I have a favour to ask."

"Speak on," said the King. "I shall grant whatever you request."

Shahrazade asked her maidservants to bring the children, of whom one was already walking, one crawling and one still suckling, and she set them down in front of the King.

"Here, my King, are your children. I ask you to release me from the sentence of death for, if I die, these boys will have no mother to raise them as they should be."

When the King heard this he wept, and gathered his sons to him.

"Shahrazade," he said, "even before you asked, I had promised myself not to have you put to death. You have shown every virtue that a woman could have. With your stories, you have taught me that others have suffered greater tribulations than I." At this, Shahrazade embraced the King, who went on, "Praise be to Allah, for He sent you to teach me that I have done a terrible wrong. I shall never stop blaming myself for the dreadful slaughter of so many innocent girls."

At once, the Wazir was sent for and was told that his daughter would become the King's legal wife and Queen. Imagine his joy that she had been spared the fate of the young women before her! So too, Shah Zaman, the King's brother, was summoned from Samarkand.

Meanwhile, the festivities began: the streets were filled with the sweet scents of burning aloe-wood and costly perfumes; the Town Crier summoned the folk to the Divan where tables were set with sweetmeats and whole sheep were roasted on spits.

For seven days and seven nights, the people of the town, both rich and poor, both high and low, feasted and drank and were reconciled with the King, though so many of them had lost their daughters during the years of slaughter.

When Shah Zaman arrived, the King told him about the stories that Shahrazade had related over a thousand nights and one night, and of their wisdom and the lessons he had learnt. And he told of his intention that these tales should be set down by the most skilled recorders of the eastern world, and that copies should be dispersed throughout the Kingdom, as an instruction to his people and to those who followed, century after century.

Shah Zaman, who had followed his brother's cruel example in Samarkand, listened in wonder. Filled with remorse, he asked if he could marry Shahrazade's younger sister, Dunyazade. The King agreed, but Shahrazade could not bear to be parted from her sister, so the King invited his brother to stay and share his palace. Accordingly, the girls' father, the Wazir, was appointed Viceroy of Samarkand in Shah Zaman's stead. There, in time, he was made Sultan by the people, who were grateful for his justice and fairness.

Now, with his brother at his side and in preparation for the

"Here, my King, are your children."

wedding ceremonies, the King distributed alms to the poor and gave rich gifts to his captains and notables. The two brides were taken to the Hammam baths, which had been scented with rose water, willow flower water, musk and ambergris. Shahrazade was dressed in a red robe stitched with golden birds and beasts, her sister Dunyazade in a robe of blue and gold. Both were decked out in ropes of pearls, rubies and diamonds, but when the King and his brother arrived at the Hammam, they thought that nothing shone as brightly as the radiant faces and flashing eyes of their brides.

Shah Zaman came to live in the palace and shared the duties of Kingship, day and day about, with his brother. And so began long years of happiness and delight for the two royal couples, and for the people they ruled over with wisdom and in peace.